HUNTING AVA

Other Books by Kiki Swinson

Playing Dirty

Notorious

Wifey

I'm Still Wifey

Life After Wifey

The Candy Shop

A Sticky Situation

Still Wifey Material

Still Candy Shopping

Wife Extraordinaire

Wife Extraordinaire Returns

Cheaper to Keep Her

Cheaper to Keep Her 2

The Score

Cheaper to Keep Her 3

Cheaper to Keep Her 4

The Mark

Cheaper to Keep Her 5

Dead on Arrival

The Black Market

The Safe House, Black Market 2

Property of the State, Black Market 3

The Deadline

Public Enemy #1

Playing with Fire

Burning Season

Where There's Smoke

Amber Alert

HUNTING AVA

KIKI SWINSON

KENSINGTON PUBLISHING CORP.
kensingtonbooks.com

This book is a work of fiction. Names, characters, businesses, organizations, places, events, and incidents either are the product of the author's imagination or are used fictitiously. Any resemblance to actual persons, living or dead, events, or locales is entirely coincidental.

To the extent that the image or images on the cover of this book depict a person or persons, such person or persons are merely models, and are not intended to portray any character or characters featured in the book.

DAFINA BOOKS are published by

Kensington Publishing Corp.
900 Third Avenue
New York, NY 10022

All Kensington Titles, Imprints, and Distributed Lines are available at special quantity discounts for bulk purchases for sales promotions, premiums, fund-raising, and educational or institutional use. Special book excerpts or customized printings can also be created to fit specific needs. For details, write or phone the office of the Kensington special sales manager: Kensington Publishing Corp., 900 Third Avenue, New York, NY 10022, attn.: Special Sales Department, Phone: 1-800-221-2647.

Library of Congress Control Number: 2025936250

ISBN: 978-1-4967-4689-4
First Kensington Hardcover Edition: October 2025

ISBN: 978-1-4967-4691-7 (ebook)

10 9 8 7 6 5 4 3 2 1

Printed in the United States of America

The authorized representative in the EU for product safety and compliance is eucomply OU, Parnu mnt 139b-14, Apt 123
Tallinn, Berlin 11317, hello@eucompliancepartner.com

HUNTING AVA

CHAPTER 1

Ava & Kevin

IT'S BEEN FOUR MONTHS SINCE MY MOVE TO HOUSTON, TEXAS, AND it has been peaceful. I brought Paulina and the kids with me and we're now living in a beautiful five-bedroom, four-bath, one-million-dollar house. It also has a three-car garage, and all the amenities to go with it. I couldn't have asked for a better home. The good thing about it is that I purchased it with cold, hard cash. I even bought myself a brand-new SUV. In fact, I picked up a $240,000 Bentley Bentayga truck. It came with all the bells and whistles, and I am enjoying the hell out of it.

My divorce from Kevin is still ongoing, but I will get through it. Since the house is on the market, I heard from the kids that he's living in Richmond with his sidepiece, Ty. I'm sure she loved it when she found out that I filed for divorce. I'm sure she was waiting with bated breath for that day to happen. He Face-times the kids every day like clockwork. He wants to see what's going on and who's around us. He knows that Paulina is with me, and I bought a bigger house. He even knows that Nick is dead. Kevin was informed a day later when the detectives stopped by our home and questioned us both about the last time we saw or spoke with Nick. When they stopped by, I had Paulina take the children out of the house for ice cream. Kevin told them the last time he spoke with Nick was the day after our kids were kidnapped. When it was my turn to speak, I told them I had stopped by his shop to see if I could borrow money for my kids' ransom. When Nick told me that he couldn't help me, I left, and that was the last time I saw him. I took it they believed what we said because they hadn't reached back out to us again for further questioning.

After the detectives left, Kevin went into interrogation mode to see if I knew anything about Nick's death, but I told him flat out that I didn't. What I told him was, Nick took me to meet the kidnappers, he handed them the money, got the kids back for me, and then we went our separate ways after that. My story seemed plausible, so I gathered that he believed me, too. No one knew what really happened—but me and Little Kevin—and I made him promise that he wouldn't tell a soul—not even his father. He said that he wouldn't tell anyone.

Thankfully, Kevin wasn't giving me any grief about the kids being in the South with me. I assumed his mistress and his new baby kept him busy to the point where our kids' absences hadn't bothered him so much, so that worked great for me.

As usual, he'd call on Saturday morning to check on the kids before Paulina took them to their soccer games. I've always tried to stay out of the way to avoid speaking with him. After finding out about the other woman and the baby, his pathetic existence really got underneath my skin. Knowing that he picked up another family behind my back was the most diabolical act of betrayal of a lifetime and I knew it was going to take me a while to get over it. There was nothing else for me to do but embrace it.

I was in my bedroom when he called my cell phone to Facetime with Little Kevin and Kamryn. Instead of answering it myself, I walked into Kamryn's bedroom, where she was, and handed her the phone.

"Hi, Daddy," she answered as I walked away and headed back into my bedroom, which was only a few feet away. I could hear the conversation clear as day.

"Hey, baby girl, what's going on?" Kevin started off.

"Nothing much. Just getting ready to go to my soccer game," Kamryn replied.

"Are you excited about it?"

"Yes, I am. I think we're gonna win this time, because the girls we are playing aren't really good."

"That's awesome. I wish I could be there to see it."

"So, when are you coming out here to see us?"

"Soon. I just have to take some time off work and then I'll take a flight out there to see you guys."

"Okay, do you want to talk to Little Kevin now?" she asked. It was apparent that she was more excited about getting ready for her soccer game than talking to her father. Kevin was used to the kids casting him to the side for outside activities, so he didn't take it personally.

"Yes, of course. Where is he?" I heard him say.

"I think he's in his room, hold on. Let me go get him," Kamryn said, and then I heard her run into the hallway, where Little Kevin was probably fishing his sports equipment out of the closet, like he did every Saturday morning.

When Little Kevin came into her room, she handed the phone to her brother. I heard Little Kevin say, "Hey, Dad."

"Hey, son, what's going on?" Kevin replied.

"Nothing much, just got my kneepads and now I'm getting my gym bag. Paulina is waiting outside in the car to take us to our games." The conversation faded out as he headed back into his bedroom with my cell phone. I didn't time their conversation, but they were on the phone for a good while, so I continued on with doing my chores. That was abruptly interrupted when Little Kevin walked into my bedroom and handed me my cell phone back.

"Dad wants to talk to you."

Instantly annoyed by the fact that Kevin wanted to speak with me, I took a deep breath and braced myself for what he had to say, while Little Kevin sped off into the opposite direction.

Now facing him via Facetime, I gave him a nonchalant expression and asked, "What do you need?"

He got straight to the point. "Is there something you wanna tell me?"

"What are you talking about?" I was becoming more irritated by the second.

"Tell Little Kevin to come back to the phone."

"For what? Just spit it out."

"Was Nick the one who kidnapped my kids?" Kevin asked me directly.

Shocked by his question, I swallowed hard on the imaginary lump in my throat and pretended not to have heard his question clearly. I calmly asked him to repeat himself.

"You heard me. Was Nick the one who kidnapped my kids?" he asked once again, with his eyes laser focused on me. Kevin and I had been together for a long time, so he knew when I was lying. I wouldn't give him direct eye contact and the palm of my hands would start to sweat uncontrollably. Today I had an edge because he couldn't see my hands, so all I had to do was keep direct eye contact with him and he'd believe me.

"Where did you get that from?" I asked, creating another stall tactic.

"Where do you think I got it from? Little Kevin just told me," he stated outright.

"I don't believe you," I said, looking him straight in the eyes.

"Call him right now. Get him to come back to the phone," Kevin demanded. I could tell that he was getting upset and losing patience with me.

"He's not here. He just walked out of the house to go to his game," I lied. I could literally hear Little Kevin downstairs rummaging around in the refrigerator, getting himself a snack to take with him. Kamryn was already in the car with Paulina.

"Ava, don't bullshit me! Why would Little Kevin volunteer and tell me that my friend Nick was the one who took him and his sister out of our house?"

"He probably said it because Nick's face was the first one he saw after he paid the guys the ransom money." My lies kept coming and my story was coming together.

"Stop it, Ava!"

"Stop what?"

"Little Kevin told me about y'all's little secret, too."

"What secret?" I pretended not to know. But deep down in my heart, I knew what Kevin was about to tell me and I instantly got sick to my stomach. I wanted to vomit right then and there, but I realized that Kevin was watching my every move, so I had to hold on to my composure.

"Since you wanna play fucking dumb, let me tell you about my son's little secret," he started off saying. His eyes doubled in size and spit spewed forth from his mouth. "His exact words, 'Dad, I wanna tell you about me and Mom's secret, but you gotta promise that you won't tell anyone else.' So I said, 'Son, I promise I won't tell a soul.' And then he went on to tell me that he heard you and Nick arguing upstairs in Nick's kitchen because you found out that he was the one who kidnapped him and his sister. Then he said that Nick started beating on you, so he ran upstairs, grabbed the gun that was on the floor, and killed Nick with it," Kevin added.

Taken aback by this whole conversation, I stood there paralyzed, and I was at a loss for words. How was I going to talk my way out of this? Little Kevin just exposed the truth to his father and now I needed to figure out how I was going to handle things going forward.

"So you don't have anything to say?" Kevin pressed me.

"What do you want me to say?" I asked. I mean, I couldn't lie and say that what Little Kevin said wasn't true, because what child at his age would conjure up a story like that?

"First of all, I want to know why you didn't tell me that Nick was the one who kidnapped my kids? And two, don't you think I should've been the first person to know that my son was the one who shot and killed him? My goodness, I am his fucking father and you're his mother, so you should've been the one to tell me right after the shit happened."

Still not knowing what to say, I stood there, trying to gather my thoughts and this pissed Kevin off. "So you're just gonna stand there and say nothing?" he spat out.

"I don't know what to say," I finally spoke up.

"Why don't you start with the reason you felt like it was okay for you not to tell me what happened the night you got my kids back? I mean, don't you think that what Little Kevin did is going to affect him for the rest of his life? That shit probably traumatized him."

"You're blowing this out of proportion. He's gonna be fine."

"How can you say that? He fucking shot and killed a man, Ava! Do you know what that does to a person's mind? Just imagine what it can do to a kid."

"I understand what you're saying, but you should've saw him when he did it. He was a natural, and after he did it, he mentioned that it felt good to protect me."

"He's a freaking child, Ava. He's not mature enough to be in tune with his feelings."

"I'm telling you, Kevin, our son is a different breed. He's gonna be fine."

"No, he's not, Ava. And I suggest that you take him to a shrink."

"Are you crazy? I am not taking him to a fucking shrink! No

one else can find out about this, because if they do, then there's a chance that our son could go to jail, and I wouldn't be able to live with that."

"If what you said was true, then he wouldn't go. It would be a case of self-defense."

"No, I can't chance it," I said with finality.

Kevin let out a long sigh. "Look, I'm gonna leave that alone for right now, but we will revisit this later."

"Yeah, whatever," I uttered, my words barely audible. Right when I lifted my free hand to press the END button, Kevin said, "Hey, wait, before you go."

"What is it?" I replied.

"I'm gonna need my part of the ransom back, now that I know that Nick was the actual kidnapper."

"What do you mean, *your* part?"

"The part that I gave you. I want that back."

"What makes you think I have it?"

"You think I'm stupid, don't you? I always wondered how you were able to pack up, relocate out of town, and purchase a new house when I was the only breadwinner in this house? And now it all makes sense to me."

I let out a nervous laugh.

"You go ahead and laugh, but I know what I'm talking about. Speaking of which, I spoke to Nick's sister, Lacey, right after he was murdered and she told me that all of Nick's money was stolen from his house, along with his computer and some other things. Now that I know you were the last one there after Nick was killed, I know you took the ransom money back. So I want my part back and you've got less than forty-eight hours to send it to me," he warned.

"Do you realize that piece of shit took our kids from us because he figured that would be the only way he was going to get back all the money that you owed him?"

"That's bullshit! Don't blame that on me!" Kevin shouted. It was obvious that he didn't want to be the blame for our children's kidnapping.

"Well, it's the truth. He said that you were a fucking loser, Kevin! And that I was stupid for leaving him to be with you. He said that I was better off with him."

"He didn't say that."

"Believe what you want, but I'm not sending you a dime. Charge it to the game! You owed it to Nick anyway."

"Listen, you bitch, if you don't send me that money, shit is going to hit the fan."

"And what does that mean?"

"Don't send me my money back and you will find out," Kevin threatened.

I chuckled. "So, whatcha gonna do? Call the cops and tell them that your son shot and killed a man?"

"Yes, and I'm gonna tell them you were there and that you coerced him into doing your dirty work for you."

"That's bullshit! I wouldn't never get Little Kevin to do that!" I roared. "If I could take that day back, I would've killed Nick my fucking self! Don't you dare say that bullshit to me again," I continued.

"Yeah, you can pretend to have wanted to save the day all you want, but I know you. And I know how conniving you can be, so save that melodrama for someone who doesn't know you. Before I go, I want you to look at a calendar and figure out when you'll be able to put my kids on a plane and send them back here to Virginia so I can spend some time with them."

"Oh, you can forget that. That'll never happen," I refuted the idea.

"And why not?"

"Do you think that I'm gonna let you take my kids around that fucking home-wrecker you're laid up with out there? I think not."

"She's not a home-wrecker. And besides, they're gonna have to meet her one day. She and I have a kid together, who is their sibling."

"Do you think I care about that kid being their sibling? It's not happening."

"Oh, it's gonna happen. And it may happen after the cops put your ass behind bars and I get full custody of the kids."

I chuckled once again because I saw where this whole conversation was going. "So you think by having this over my head, you're gonna get full custody of the kids? Fat chance, buddy!"

"You can laugh all you want, because for one, there's no judge in the court system that's gonna prevent me from having my kids around Ty and my daughter. And two, if you don't send me my money, this whole situation will get ugly, and I will get full custody when it's all said and done."

"We'll see about that," I told him, and then I abruptly ended the Facetime call.

After I ended our call, I stood there pissed off at the idea that he threatened me about the ransom money. Then, on top of that, the audacity of him wanting me to put the kids on a flight so they could go and visit him in Virginia so that he could parade his fucking side chick and baby around them. Was he crazy? My kids aren't gonna feel comfortable with that dynamic over there. They're just now getting adjusted to the idea that we're going through a divorce. Allow us to get over this first hurdle and then, maybe after that, we can address the fact that he fucked around on me and had that baby. But until then, we're gonna do things my way.

Still reeling from the thought of that bastard threatening me with the cops and taking my kids away from me, I couldn't do anything else but toss my phone on the bed and slump down on the edge of it. I figured the only thing to do was wait it out and see what happens next. And if push came to shove, to keep him from taking my kids from me, I'd end his life for sure. Because I refuse to let another soul take my kids away from me and live to tell about it.

Not now. Not ever.

And that includes their father.

CHAPTER 2
Kevin & Ty

"THINK SHE'S GOING TO SEND YOUR PART OF THE RANSOM BACK?" Ty asked me when she entered the living room, where I was sitting down on the sofa.

"I take it you heard my conversation?" I said.

"Yep, I heard every word," she replied, sitting down next to me.

"Can you believe that shit?"

"Which part?"

"All of it. She literally kept that entire night a secret from me. And if it wasn't for my son, I would've never known what happened. What kind of mother is she?"

"I can't tell you what kind of mother she is, but I can say that I would've never allowed my child to do that."

"I couldn't, either."

"So, how do you feel about him killing your friend?"

"Well, it's obvious that he really wasn't my friend, especially after finding out he was the one who kidnapped my kids. Besides that, I feel bad for my son, because knowing that you were the cause of someone else's death can be traumatizing, especially for a kid his age. And for his mother to not have made me privy to that information has my blood boiling."

"You think she stole money from that guy?"

"Absolutely. And now that I know it, I want my money back."

"How much did you give her?" Ty wanted to know.

"Over six hundred thousand."

"Wow! That's a lot of money."

"Shit! Tell me about it."

"Think she's gonna give it to you?"

"She has no choice."

"What are you gonna do if she doesn't? Are you gonna really call the cops on her?"

"No. I'm not."

"Then why did you say it?"

"Because I'm upset. I figured that if I told her that, it would put pressure on her to send me my money," I replied.

"That threat would definitely put pressure on me. In fact, it would scare the shit out of me."

"That was the point. But she's such a hard-ass, it probably went right over her head. See, all the years I've known her, she's never been really scared of anything. I guess it's because she's lived a hard life of growing up poor and then living a life of crime."

"Oh, wow! So she's seen a thing or two, huh?"

"Oh, absolutely. When I came into her life, I took her away from that lifestyle."

"Well, they say that you can take a person out of the ghetto, but you can't necessarily take the ghetto out of them."

I let out a long sigh. "You can say that again."

Ty leaned in my direction and started massaging my shoulders. "You look so tense," she commented.

"After having that conversation with Ava, my body feels more than tense," I told her as she jolted my body back and forth. I tried to relax, but the thoughts in my head wouldn't allow me.

"I'm sure. The topic of conversation itself was a lot. I couldn't imagine finding out that our daughter, at your son's age, killed someone, and the other parent kept that from me. No disrespect, but she needs to see a shrink herself, thinking that way of parenting is okay. She shouldn't have those kids in her custody full-time. Ava clearly demonstrated that she doesn't make the best decisions as a parent. What Little Kevin did is considered a crime, and whether she knows it or not, she's now involved, and if the cops were to find out, she could be charged with accessory after the fact," Ty expressed.

I sat there for a moment and thought about what she said, and Ty was right. Ava could get charged for her involvement, and maybe if I remind her of that, she wouldn't have a choice but to send me my money back. I guess, I will find out.

"Can I ask you something?" I asked.

"Sure."

"How did you feel when you heard Ava saying that she didn't want the kids around you and the baby?"

Ty chuckled as if Ava's comment alone was amusing; then she said, "Just know that I didn't take it personal because I know those words came from a place of hurt. She's bitter that you have another family, so it's gonna take her some time to come to terms with it and move on. To be perfectly honest, I'd probably feel the same way if I were in her shoes."

"So you weren't offended at all?"

Ty smiled. "Of course not. I told you, I'd probably feel the same way. But knowing me, I don't think I would give you the satisfaction of knowing it. I'd keep it to myself."

"You'd really keep it to yourself?"

"Of course, I would. I'm a very prideful person. I'd die first before I let you see me hurt, especially behind another woman."

"Wow! Thanks for sharing," I said, and then I dropped the subject about Ava and started talking about our future plans together. "Wanna get married right after my divorce is final?"

Ty's face lit up. "Of course, baby, I would love that. Oh, my God! Are you proposing to me?" she asked with excitement.

I chuckled. "No! No! No! I'm not proposing just yet. I just wanted to know if we were on the same page about when was a good time to tie the knot."

"Baby, none of that matters. I'm just so excited that you're thinking about making me your wife."

"How could I not think about it? You gave me a beautiful daughter. And besides, we're like a match made from heaven. You complete me, Ty," I said with sincerity.

"Awww . . . really? Thank you so much, baby! I really appreciate you saying that," she replied. Then she leaned in and gave me an intimate kiss on the lips. Sparks started flying everywhere and my manhood stood up.

"Come on, let's go in the room and have some fun before the baby wakes up," I suggested.

Without saying a word, Ty grabbed me by the hand and led me into the bedroom.

It's been thirty-six hours since I last spoke to Ava. I've tried calling her cell phone, but she is not answering. Unfortunately, my children don't have phones of their own yet, so I'm unable to reach out to them. Because of Ava's actions, I see that she doesn't have any plans to return my part of the kids' ransom money. Now I have no other choice but to take matters into my own hands. Things are about to get really ugly, and she will regret this day.

Without further hesitation I picked up my cell phone to call Nick's sister, Lacey, who resides in Los Angeles with her husband, Maceo. They have their own chop shop business going on out there. I was sure she'd be interested in finding out who stole her brother Nick's belongings. Maybe after I bring her up to speed about the latest developments, she may reward me with a finder's fee for the information that I'm about to lay on her.

"Hey, Lace, what's going on?" I asked after she answered her phone.

"Hey, Kevin, nothing much. What's going on with you?" she replied.

"Just calling to check up on you, make sure you're all right." I started off the conversation casually, trying to gauge her mood. I knew Lace was a crazy bitch and she would go off the handle at the drop of a dime.

"Kevin, all I can do is take it one day at a time," she said nonchalantly.

"Are you coming back on this side anytime soon?"

"Well, I was thinking about coming back that way next week so that I can tie up some loose ends with business affairs that Nick started up before his death. Why you ask?"

"Because I need to talk to you about something very serious."

"What's it about?" She seemed curious.

"It's about Nick."

"What about him?" she asked, the tone of her voice changed. I could tell that I had gotten her attention.

"I can't say it over the phone," I told her, using an evasive tone. I was sure after doing that, she'd know this was a serious matter.

"I'll tell you what, go get a burner phone and call me back on this number," she instructed. She was very eager to hear what I had to say.

"Okay, give me twenty minutes."

"All right," she said, and then we ended the call.

Immediately after hanging up, I shoved my cell phone down in my pants pocket. I grabbed my car keys, left the house, and drove to the nearest corner store to purchase a throwaway phone. With the phone in hand, I sat in my car, then powered the phone on and activated it. Within minutes the phone was working, so I dialed Lacey's phone number. She answered on the first ring.

"Hey, what do you have for me?" She didn't hesitate at all to ask.

"Remember you said you'd pay a finder's fee if someone told you who was responsible for Nick's death and the items stolen from his house?"

"Yeah," she responded, and by her tone I could tell that I had piqued her interest.

"First of all, what's the finder's fee?" I wanted to know.

"If you're about to tell me who murdered my brother, I'll pay two hundred grand for that. If you're able to show me where I can find them, then I'll throw in another fifty grand on top of that. And if that same person has my brother's computer and his money, I will pay a cool million with no problem."

"So you're saying that if I give you all that information, you'll give me one-point-two million dollars?" I asked her. I wanted clarity.

"Yes, Kevin, I would. Now tell me who killed my brother," she demanded to know.

I took a deep breath and exhaled. I knew that after I gave her this information, there was no turning back. I wouldn't be able to recant anything I was about to say.

"Who are they?" she pressed me.

I cleared my throat and said, "It was one person."

"Who?" She stood firm.

"My wife, Ava," I finally said.

I swear, after I uttered her name, I could hear a pin drop on the other end of the line. There was complete silence. When Lacey and I began our conversation, I could hear her breathing, but now nothing was audible.

"Ava killed my brother?" she asked. Her voice instantly became menacing. It almost sounded like she was a mechanical robot.

"Yes," I assured her.

"And how do you know this?"

"Because she told me."

"And what exactly did she tell you?"

"She told me that Nick was the one who kidnapped my children. The reason why he kidnapped them was because making me pay a ransom was the only way he was going to get the money back that I owed him . . ."

"That's bullshit! My brother had nothing to do with that! He wouldn't have ever done anything like that. He loved your children like they were his own. He was their godfather, for God's sake," she interjected. She really took offense at that accusation.

"No, it's true, Lacey. My son was the one who told me about it first. When Little Kevin told me, he made me promise that I would keep it a secret, and not to tell his mom that I knew about it."

"So he's trying to protect her?"

"Well, of course, but you know why she told him not to tell me?"

"Yeah, because if you knew she was the one who murdered him, then you would've figured out she was also the one who stole his money and computer."

"Exactly."

"Have you confronted her with this?"

"Yes, I asked her about it, but she denied it." I lied to Lacey. I couldn't let on that I blackmailed Ava in exchange for getting my part of the ransom back. Lacey would look at me differently and assume that I was okay with what happened to Nick. I wanted to distance myself from that situation at all costs. When you had a beef with Nick or his family, there was always hell to pay. Throughout the years, I witnessed so many get hurt and even murdered by the hands of these people. They were notorious for making people pay for their bad deeds, and knowing this, I never wanted to put myself in a position to be on the receiving end of their reign of terror.

"Where are you now?" Lacey wanted to know.

"I'm home."

"Is she there with you?"

"No, I live in Richmond. And she just relocated to Houston."

"Oh, wow! When did that happen?"

"After we got the kids back, she filed for divorce, packed up her and the kids' things, and moved out of the house we shared. After she left, I moved to Richmond."

"Who's at your house now?"

"No one. We put it on the market. So, hopefully, we'll get to sell it before our divorce is final."

"Do you have her address in Houston?"

"Yes, it's on the divorce filing packet that I just recently received."

"Well, text it to me and I'll handle things from there."

"Wait, hold up, what are you going to do?" I asked her. I knew Lacey was ruthless and she'd put a contract out on someone's head without even blinking twice. I just needed to know what she was planning to do so that I could make sure my kids weren't around when she made her move.

"Come on now, Kevin, you know I can't tell you that."

"I understand that, but my kids are there with her and I can't let anything happen to them," I pointed out.

"Well, allow me to promise you that nothing will happen to your children. They will be perfectly safe," she assured me. However, her assurance didn't give me any peace of mind because I knew my son. If by any chance Little Kevin was around and he felt like his mother's life was being threatened, he'd do anything to protect her. I mean, look at what he did to Nick. Now I can't disclose that information to Lacey because she may want to do something to my son. I figured the best thing for me to do was fly out there and take my kids out of the house before Lacey sends her goons after Ava. That would be my best bet.

"Hey, listen, I'll tell you what. I'm gonna fly out there and get my kids out of there before the shit hits the fan," I volunteered.

"Be my guest," Lacey commented.

"So, when am I going to be compensated?" I wanted to know.

"Right after we deal with your wife and retrieve my brother's things."

"Can I get an advance?"

"Are you low on cash?"

"Kinda, sort of."

"Well, text me your banking information and I'll wire thirty grand tomorrow."

"All right, thanks."

"Don't mention it. And look, don't alert your wife about what's coming her way, because if you do, we're gonna come after you next," she warned.

"Trust me, I won't."

"Good, now if you hear that she's leaving town anytime soon, let me know."

"Okay," I replied, my mood turning sour at the possibility of me getting hurt.

"Hey, don't sound so down. Look at it this way, since your divorce hasn't been finalized yet, after she's gone, everything that she owns will be yours," Lacey stated, and then she chuckled.

She had a point, but I wasn't in the mood to laugh after she threatened me. And when she realized that, she said, "Hey, listen, call me if anything changes, and, in the meantime, I'm gonna wire you this money, okay?"

"Okay. Thanks."

"Don't mention it," she said, and then we both ended the call.

Immediately after the call ended, I tossed my phone on the passenger seat of my car and sat there in disbelief. I honestly couldn't believe that I just ratted my wife out to Nick's people, and in a couple of hours from now, there was going to be a hit out on her. And it was all in the name of money. When she's gone, I'd be getting full custody of my kids and the entire payment from the sale of the house.

What a win-win situation I was in. Damn! I just hit the lottery!

CHAPTER 3

Lacey & Maceo

"KEVIN JUST CALLED ME BACK AND YOU WON'T BELIEVE WHAT HE told me," I started off saying after I entered the office of my husband Maceo's chop shop. He was sitting behind his desk, looking at a magazine of million-dollar antique cars. He looked up from the magazine and gave me his undivided attention.

"What did he say?"

"He told me who killed Nick."

Maceo sat up in his chair. "Who?"

"That bitch Ava!"

Maceo shot up from his chair. "I fucking knew it! I knew she had something to do with his murder!" he screeched as his nostrils flared up.

"She has his computer, too."

"What are we waiting for? Let's go and get it." Maceo abruptly shot around his desk.

"Slow down, baby! She's not in Virginia anymore."

"Then where is she?"

"She's in Houston now."

"Since when?"

"She packed up and left right after she murdered my brother."

"Do you have an address for her?"

"Kevin is going to text it to me."

"Who do you want me to put on this?"

"Call Nasir, but let him know that we're gonna accompany him this time around."

"Are you sure that's wise?" Maceo wanted to know. Normally, when we assign hits, we never accompany our hit man when they go after the targets.

"Let me tell you something, I will not give up the opportunity to see that bitch squirm around like the fucking dirty snake she is."

"Look, I know you hate her guts, but we've gotta do this smart."

"And we will."

"So, when do you want to move on this?"

"By the end of the week."

"Let's do it," Maceo said, retrieving his phone from his front pants pocket. I watched him dial the number of our mercenary. Their conversation wasn't long at all. Maceo basically told Nasir that we had a job for him, and we needed it executed by the end of the week. He agreed and assured us he would get with us in a few days on the specifics. After Maceo ended the call, he looked at me and smiled.

"What's the smile for?" I asked.

"Because we're about to make this bitch pay for what she did to your brother."

"Yes, that is something to smile about. More importantly, we're gonna get his things back and that's what counts at this phase in the game."

Maceo's smile widened. "I couldn't agree more," he sided with me as he slid his cell phone back into his pocket.

"Hey, I told Kevin I would wire him some money."

"How much?"

"Thirty grand," I answered.

"You're not gonna send it through our business account, are you?"

"Of course not, silly. I'm gonna send it through one of our shell company accounts on Monday."

"Look, I know Kevin was your brother's childhood best friend, but do you trust him not to rat us out to the cops after we kill his wife? I mean, that is the mother of his children."

"Why would he wanna risk going to jail?"

"Because they could cut him a deal," Maceo pointed out. "I think we should get rid of him. That'll eliminate him from coming back to us later and trying to blackmail us for more money."

"I promised to give him a million after we completed the hit on Ava and confiscated the money and computer back."

"You know we can't do that."

"And we're not."

"How do you propose we pull that off?"

"We're gonna clip him right after we finish Ava off."

"What about the kids?"

"What about 'em?"

"Are we gonna get rid of them, too?"

I chuckled loudly. My husband had a tendency of going to extreme measures at times. "Come on now, Maceo, when have we ever killed kids?"

"So, what are we going to do with them then?"

"We're gonna leave them tied up somewhere and let the foster care system deal with them later."

"Cool," Maceo said nonchalantly.

"You know, I'm wondering how much of Nick's money Ava has spent."

"It can't be that much. Nick hasn't been dead that long."

"Kevin told me that she bought a new house. And it wouldn't surprise me if she bought a new car, too."

"Whatever she spent, it couldn't be more than a couple of million. She's a smart girl and she would want to keep a low profile, especially since the cops are still looking for your brother's killer."

"Remember, we're talking about Ava, the same chick who tried to spend all of Nick's stash money after she found out he cheated on her when he got locked up," I reminded him.

"Well, I guess you got a point there. So let's hope she didn't try to do the same thing this time around."

"We'll see."

CHAPTER 4

Ty & Whitney

KEVIN CALLED TO TELL ME THAT HE'D BE HOME IN AN HOUR, SO I decided to start dinner. As I began to stir the sauce in the pot, the aroma of garlic, onions, and tomatoes filled the kitchen. Tonight I was going to surprise him with his favorite dish, Marry Me Chicken. While I chopped up the fresh basil, my cell phone began to ring, and when I looked down at it near the chopping board, I noticed the caller was my bestie, Whitney. I quickly slid the ANSWER button over to the right and said hello after wiping my hands with the kitchen towel.

"Hey, girl, whatcha doing?" she responded.

"Cooking."

"Cooking what?"

"Kevin's favorite chicken dish."

"Oh, you must be making Marry Me Chicken," Whitney guessed, her voice tinged with excitement.

I chuckled. "You got it," I replied. "So, how was your vacay in Jamaica? Tell me everything," I asked, smiling despite the pang of envy at Whitney's tropical adventure.

"It was incredible! The water was beautiful, the food fantastic, the rum out of this world, and the vibe—it was like living in a postcard! We did every water sport under the sun. We laid out on the beach, and danced with the locals," Whitney gushed. "And Todd was such a sweetheart. You gotta see this beautiful necklace he got me."

"Sounds like someone might be pregnant," I joked.

"Come on now, you know I'm not *that* crazy. Trust me, we still use condoms."

"Wait, how long have you guys been together now?"

"A year and a couple of months."

"And you two are still using condoms?"

"Yes, ma'am. That's only because he's made it clear that we're not exclusive. He makes it very clear that we're only dating. So I'm cool with it."

"Well, at least he's honest."

"And I can't do anything but respect it."

"So it sounds like Jamaica was a blast!"

"Yes, it was," Whitney assured me. "So, what's been going on with you and the family?"

"Kevin, the baby, and I are good. But, girl, some true-crime drama dropped a couple of days ago, on Saturday, and Kevin is still reeling from it."

"What happened?" Whitney asked, her curiosity piqued.

I paused for a second trying to debate how much of this information I should divulge about Nick's murderer. Then I figured that Whitney was my confidante and I've known her almost my whole life. She was the only person in this world that I could trust with anything, so I decided it was safe to let the cat out of the bag. "You remember that whole kidnapping incident with Kevin's kids, right?" I lowered my voice.

"Yes, I remember, but why are we whispering? It's just you and the baby there, right?" she asked.

I thought about it for a second and realized that I was alone, so there wasn't a need to be whispering. I laughed out loud. "My bad," I commented. Then I said, "Well, Kevin and I finally found out who the kidnapper was."

"Who?"

"His freaking best friend, Nick."

"No fucking way!"

"Yes, way. And it gets more complicated than that," I said, recalling the recent revelation.

"What is it?" Whitney urged, sensing my seriousness.

"So Kevin calls his son, Little Kevin, to check on him and his sister. While they're talking, Little Kevin decides that he wants to tell Big Kevin a secret that his mother, Ava, told him not to tell anyone. Before Little Kevin tells his father what the secret is, he makes his dad promise not to say anything to his mother. Big Kevin promises that he won't. So, after getting that out of the way, Little Kevin drops a bombshell and proceeds to tell his father that Nick was the one who kidnapped him and his sister, and when Ava found out about it, she and Nick got into a fight and he started beating her up. When Little Kevin saw Nick beating up his mom, he grabbed a gun that he saw on the floor of Nick's house and used it to shoot him," I revealed, the words feeling surreal as I said them out loud.

There was a stunned silence at the other end of the line for about thirty seconds before Whitney finally spoke. "Wait, so Little Kevin is the one who killed Nick?" she asked, her voice mixed with disbelief and concern.

"Yup."

"Oh, my God! What are they going to do?" Whitney wanted to know.

I immediately recounted the conversation Kevin and I had after it had completely registered in his mind what his son had done. Also, as Whitney listened intently, I told her that he really didn't have a solid solution to that incident.

"Didn't the cops come to talk to them after they found that guy's body?"

"Yes, they did."

"So, is he going to call them back and tell them what he knows now?"

"He threatened Ava that he was going to do it and get her for accessory to murder after the fact, but I doubt if he goes through with it."

"Yeah, he could. But doing that would also jeopardize his son's freedom. With the way the judicial system is run now, they'd probably try that baby as an adult."

"So, what would you do in a situation like that?"

"I don't know," Whitney answered softly, not sure what to say. "How are you feeling about all of this? And what advice did you offer Kevin?"

"I really didn't know what to say, either. I do know that if I were that child's mother, I would not have ever put him in a situation like that in the first place."

"You know what? As I sit here and think about it, I'm wondering how the little boy is handling all of this. That had to have been a traumatic experience for him," Whitney pointed out.

"I asked the same question. But Ava is acting like he's doing fine."

"Girl, I don't believe that crap. Unless you're a cold-blooded murderer, you're gonna feel some type of guilt or go through a stage of depression to the point where you'll spiral into your own personal hell of psychiatric issues or suicide," Whitney explained.

"Well, let's hope it doesn't get to that point."

"They might want to take him to therapy or something. Because if they don't, and they sweep this underneath the rug, we may wake up one day and that little boy could turn into a serial killer or a professional hit man," she added.

"Damn! I didn't even think about it like that."

"Well, you better. Because who knows? You could mess around and piss him off one day when he comes to visit, and when you lay down and close your eyes, he could kill you right while you sleep."

Whitney warned me in such an alarming manner, it made the hairs on my neck stand up. I instantly thought of Little Kevin going into Annabelle's bedroom and killing her, too, just because she came from me. Oh, my God! That would be such a horrible scene and it gave me an eerie feeling. I immediately shook it off and said, "Kevin and I are gonna have a long talk when he gets here tonight."

"And you should," Whitney agreed. "And on that note, I'm gonna let you get back to cooking. Call me if you need me."

"I will, girl," I assured her, and then we ended the call.

While I continued to cook, I thought about all the types of unsettling situations that could happen in this house if Kevin doesn't get Little Kevin the help he needs, and they didn't end well. I know one thing, I have to protect my daughter, if nothing else, so if Kevin doesn't do anything about Little Kevin, I will step in and call the homicide hotline myself.

CHAPTER 5

Kevin & Ty

When I walked through the front door of my house on Monday, Ty had the entire place smelling good. I dropped my briefcase down on the floor and headed straight to the kitchen. Upon entering, I noticed Ty garnishing the chicken with parsley.

"Hey, babe. Dinner smells amazing." I greeted her with a smile as I proceeded toward her. As soon as I got within arm's reach of Ty, I leaned in and kissed her on the lips.

"Thank you," Ty replied as she grabbed a couple of plates from the cabinet.

"Where's Annabelle?" I wanted to know.

"When she woke up from her nap, I had my mother come by and get her for a couple of hours so that we could get some alone time to talk."

"Oh, cool," I said, heading over to the sink to wash my hands. Immediately after I was done, I sat down at the table and watched Ty as she plated our food. "So, how was your day?" I engaged her more.

"My day was good. I was able to wash all the clothes and dust the entire downstairs. I was also able to rearrange Annabelle's entire bedroom. You know, I've been trying to do that for weeks now," she explained as she placed the utensils down on the table next to our food.

"So, what's on your mind?" I didn't hesitate to ask. It seemed like there was an elephant in the room and I wanted to address it now.

Ty looked up at the table and met my gaze after she sat down in the chair across from me. "It's about your son, Little Kevin," her voice was steady, but tinged with concern.

"What about him? Did something happen?" Instantly I became alarmed.

"No! No! I was just thinking about the situation with your best friend, Nick, and how it could possibly affect Little Kevin. I figured that if he doesn't get any professional help, it could come back and bite all of us one day."

"Come back and bite us how?" I asked, my expression hardened slightly as a flicker of defensiveness invaded my facial features.

Ty sighed as frustration seemed to simmer beneath her calm exterior. "Look, Kevin, your son murdered your best friend. This isn't something that we can sweep underneath the rug. He's gonna need therapy—someone who can help him process what he has done."

"I know you're worried about him, and I kind of agree with you, but Ava doesn't want to involve outsiders."

"Do you realize that if you don't get him the proper help, he could one day turn into a serial killer? Or worse, he could get upset with me one day and try to off me." Ty's voice rose slightly, her concern turned into exasperation.

"Come on now, Ty, you're taking this out of proportion. My son is not going to turn into a serial killer. He's gonna be perfectly fine," I assured her, trying to downplay Little Kevin's actions.

Ty continued to press the issue. "You do know that by ignoring the problem, it won't go away. We can't just pretend that it never happened."

"I'm not pretending, Ty. I'm only protecting him. And I know what's best for him," I insisted, my tone remained firm as my jaw clenched.

Ty shook her head, her patience wearing thin. "Well, I'll tell you what, since you don't want to get him help, then he can't come here anymore."

My eyes immediately widened in disbelief. "What? Ty, he's my son. He's gonna always be welcome here."

"Not if he's gonna pose a danger to himself, or me and Annabelle," Ty retorted, her resolve hardening. "I refuse to risk our safety because you and his mother don't want to get him any help."

"I'm the one who suggested the psychiatric help in the beginning, but she shot me down," I reminded her.

"You're his father, right?"

"Of course, I am. What kind of question is that?"

"Well, then act like it. Take control of that situation before I do," Ty threatened.

"And what does that mean?"

"Try me and you and Ava will both find out," she warned me with her teeth clenched.

The tension in the room became noticeable as we stared at each other, both unwilling to back down. Finally I spoke, my voice edged with frustration. "Fine, Ty. I'll talk to Ava one more time about it, and if she's still showing some resistance, then I'll handle it on my own."

"And I appreciate that gesture more than you know." Ty's voice softened, and I could tell that I was making headway with her.

I cracked a smile. "Good, now we can eat," I suggested, hoping this would lighten the mood up even more.

She smiled back. "Sure, let's eat before it gets cold."

As we dug into our food, all you could hear was the clanging sounds of forks hitting the plates, scooping up the food, and then chewing followed. While I sat there and pretended to enjoy this moment eating with my girlfriend, I couldn't fight off the weight of our disagreement pressing down on me. So, as I contemplated my next move, whether that would be calling Ava, or flying out to talk to her in person, or simply allowing Lacey and Maceo to complete their mission, I got an uneasy feeling settling inside of me. Then I realized that I was in an uncomfortable place. I figured that regardless if Ava ended up dead or not, Little Kevin would have to carry the weight of the murder and there's no guarantee that any psychiatrist will keep that information confidential after he opens up to them. So, where would that leave him and me?

Damn! I've got a lot to think about, and if I don't do the right thing by my son, everything could fall apart for him. Not to mention, if I didn't work this situation out with him, there was a chance that I could lose Ty forever. And I can't allow that to happen, either. So, what must I do?

After dinner, Ty hopped in her car and drove over to her mother's house to get Annabelle, while I sat in my home office with my cell phone clutched tightly in my hand. For two days I had been trying to contact Ava, but there had been no answer. Each time the phone rang endlessly, echoing in my ears like an unanswered plea. I had left voice messages, texts, and even tried video calls, but nothing happened. There was no doubt in my mind that her silence was deliberate.

Frustration and worry gnawed at my mind as I scrolled through my contact list in my phone, stopping at a familiar name—Paulina—my former nanny and housekeeper, who was now living with Ava. I hesitated for a moment and wondered if she changed her phone number after the move to Texas. Without further thought I pressed the CALL button and, to my surprise, the phone started ringing. My heart instantly started pounding with a mix of anticipation and anxiety. Finally I heard a click on the other end, which signaled a connection.

"Hello," Paulina answered, her voice sounding hesitant.

"Paulina, how are you? It's Kevin," I said, trying to keep my voice steady despite how I was feeling on the inside.

"Oh, hi, Mr. Frost. Um, it's been a while. How are you?" Paulina replied, her tone cautious.

"I'm . . . I'm not too good, Paulina. I've been trying to reach Ava and the kids, and she won't answer her phone," I admitted, my words coming out in a rush.

"I'm sorry to hear that," she apologized.

"No need to apologize. Do you know where she is? Are the kids with her?" I pressed.

Paulina hesitated, clearly caught off guard by my sudden barrage of questions. "Um, well, I believe she took the kids to the park. Maybe they're out there having a good time, and she forgot to check her phone." Her answer was weak.

My eyebrows furrowed in disbelief. "The park? For days without a word? That's not like her, Paulina. You can tell me the truth. Is she trying to keep the kids away from me?" I pressured her for answers.

"No, she wouldn't ever do that . . ." Paulina tried to explain.

"Then what is it? You don't have to lie to me. These are my kids we're talking about," I reminded her.

Before Paulina could respond, I heard a door burst open, and then I heard footsteps storming across the floor. "Who are you talking to?" I heard Ava's voice fill the air.

"Mr. Frost," I heard Paulina reply.

Without warning I heard what I believed to be Ava grabbing Paulina's phone from her hand. "What the hell do you want, Kevin?" Ava shouted. Her voice was sharp, and I could hear an undertone of irritation.

"Wait, don't act like you got an attitude with me. I should be the one upset right now. I've been calling you for two days now and I got no response from you. I don't know if you or the kids are all right. Nothing," I retorted. My own frustrations were bubbling to the surface.

"You think calling Paulina is the solution? You've been verbally abusive to her in the past, and recently you're being disrespectful to me, which is why I put your ass on the back burner and refuse to answer your calls."

After I heard Ava's reasoning, I went into a rage, feeling undermined and defensive all at once. "Don't try to blame me for your actions. Do you realize what your actions have put me through?" I yelled.

"You wanna talk about actions? Let's talk about what your actions have done to me and our family!" she shouted back.

I knew she was referring to my infidelity, but this wasn't the time to talk about that. We had more important things to discuss, and Little Kevin's dilemma was one of them. "Look, Ava, I didn't call to start an argument with you. I called to find out why you weren't answering my calls or texts and to see if you guys are okay. That's it."

"Well, you're talking to me now, so you know that we're all right."

"Where are the kids?" I wondered aloud.

"They just came into the house and they're getting ready for dinner."

I looked down at my wristwatch. The time read: 7:32. "This time of the night?" I questioned her.

"Yes, *this* time of the night. We're an hour behind you, Kevin. It's only a bit after six-thirty here. I picked up a pizza on our way home and they're gonna eat it."

"Can I speak with them really quick if you don't mind?" I asked as nicely as I could. Ava had the ball in her court, so I had to play her game until the tables turned in my favor.

"Hold on," she said abruptly. "Little Kevin, Kamryn, your dad is on the phone," Ava announced as I heard her moving about.

Seconds later, I heard running and then a shuffling sound as I waited anxiously to speak with my kids. It was apparent that the phone was being passed to someone else's hand because the line crackled with a faint echo and then I heard my son's voice. "Hello, Dad," he said, his words slightly slurred with fatigue.

"Hey, son," I replied, relief flooding my tone. "How was your day?"

Little Kevin yawned. "Mom took me and Kamryn to the skate park after school."

"Did you have fun?"

"Yeah, and I met some new friends."

"Awesome!" I said, smiling despite the situation. "Did your sister skate, too?"

"No, Mom had her in the swings and monkey bars area of the park."

"Sounds like you're tired."

"Yeah, I am. I'm hungry, too. Mom picked up a pizza for dinner on the way home."

"Pizza sounds good. Make sure you don't eat too much."

"I won't," Little Kevin said, sounding more fatigued than ever. "I love you."

"I love you, too, champ," I replied warmly. "Now, can you put your sister on the phone?"

"Sure, Dad." There was a shuffling noise, and then Kamryn's voice came on the line.

"Daddy?" Kamryn's voice was more energetic than her brother's and it was filled with love.

"Yes, sweetheart, it's me," I said softly. "How was your day?"

"It was good," Kamryn replied. "Mommy took us to the park, and we got ice cream, too."

I smiled at the thought of my daughter's joy. "Sounds like you had a lot of fun."

"I did. And Mommy said that we can go back in a few days."

"Sweet! So, is everything good with you?"

"Yes."

"Met any new friends yet?"

"I have one friend named Samantha, but Mommy hasn't allowed me to hang out at her house yet. She said that she wants to keep me and Little Kevin with her at all times because of what happened to us back in Virginia."

"Well, you can't blame her, honey. Your mother and I cried every night that you guys were away from us." I sided with Ava because I had to admit that after our last scare, we can't be too careful about the safety of our kids.

"I cried, too. But Little Kevin didn't."

Hearing my baby girl tell me that my son hadn't cried while they were away from us made me more concerned than ever about this murder incident, and I knew it was imperative that I have another conversation with Ava about getting our son help.

I heard Ava shout in the background. "Kammy, you gotta eat before your food gets cold."

"Hey, Daddy, Mommy says it's time to eat," Kamryn said.

"Okay, baby, I love you. Now give the phone to your mommy so I can speak to her before I hang up," I instructed her.

"Okay, love you," she said. "Mommy, Daddy wanna talk to you," she yelled as I heard the movement of her footsteps.

"Tell him, I'll call him back tomorrow," I heard Ava say to Kammy, and this immediately pissed me off.

"Daddy, Mommy said—" Kamryn started to say, but I cut her off in midsentence.

"No, tell her to get on the phone now," I demanded. "Never mind, honey, just put me on speakerphone," I snapped in frustration.

"Okay," she replied. "Mommy, Daddy wants me to put him on speakerphone," Kamryn announced to her mother, and then I heard more shuffling noises.

"Are you deaf? Didn't I say I would call you back tomorrow?" Ava's voice boomed through the phone line.

"I just wanted to ask you a question," I told her.

Ava sighed heavily. "What is it?"

"I think we need to talk about Little Kevin's situation again," I replied.

"Look, there's nothing to talk about. I've already made my mind up. Now leave it alone and I'll talk to you later," Ava said to me, and then she abruptly disconnected our call.

My heart sank at the dismissive behavior. I wanted to react to it, but it was too late. She had already ended the call, keeping me from going off on her. I sat back in my chair and hung my head low. Something inside of me wanted to call Paulina's phone back, but I knew no one was going to answer. Ava doesn't know it yet, but I'm going to have my way—whether she wants me to or not. My son will get the help he needs. So now I guess it's time to get Ava's father involved. Maybe he will be able to talk some sense into her.

I sat there for a second before dialing Arthur's number. He and I hadn't spoken to each other in months. After Ava told him about Ty and the baby, our relationship had become strained. I know that I may be the last person he'd want to talk to, but tonight we're going to have to put those differences aside for the sake of Little Kevin.

After several minutes of hesitation, I finally dialed Ava's father's number, each ring echoing in the silent room like a reminder of unresolved tensions.

"Hello." Ava's father's voice came through, guarded yet curious.

"Hi, Arthur, it's Kevin," I said, my voice tinged with regret.

There was a palpable pause at the other end, as if Arthur was processing the unexpected call. "I know who it is. How can I help you?" he finally asked, his tone cooler than I remembered.

"Arthur, I know we haven't been on the best of terms, considering everything that's going on with Ava and me," I started, choosing my words carefully. "But I need to talk to you about something very important."

Arthur scoffed, the bitterness evident in his voice. "What is it this time?"

I sighed, frustration mingling with remorse. "I'm calling to talk to you about Little Kevin," I replied, trying to keep my emotions in check.

Arthur remained silent for a second, a heavy tension filled the air. "What's going on?" he finally asked, his voice softening slightly.

I took a deep breath, bracing myself for the difficult conversation ahead. "Remember the kidnapping incident?" I started off.

"How can I not."

"Well, I just found out that something happened right after the kids were given back to Ava. And what I was told, it's not good."

"I'm waiting," Arthur replied sarcastically. It was apparent that I was taking too long to tell him what I knew.

"Little Kevin shot and killed the guy who kidnapped him and his sister," I blurted out suddenly.

A stunned silence followed, broken only by the sound of Ava's father's sharp inhale. "Are you serious?"

"Yes, I'm afraid so," I said reluctantly.

"How did you find out about this?" he demanded to know, his tone laced with shock and disbelief.

"Little Kevin told me the other day, but he made me promise that I would keep it a secret."

"So, does Ava know about this?"

"Of course, she does. She was there. She's the one who told him not to tell me."

"Well, why in the hell didn't she call and tell me?" he wanted to know.

"I don't know, maybe she was trying to protect you," I replied, my own guilt weighing heavily on me. "But that's not why I'm telling you this. I called you because I need your help."

Arthur was quiet for a moment, processing the shocking revelation. "What kind of help do you need, Kevin?" he asked, his voice softer now.

"I need you to talk some sense into Ava. She's resistant to getting Little Kevin the help he needs. She's afraid the cops will eventually arrest him, and he'll end up in jail."

"I'll call her," he said firmly. "I'll make her understand that this is about our grandson's well-being, not about avoiding consequences."

I instantly felt a weight lift off my shoulders, grateful for the support despite our past differences. "Thank you," I said with genuine gratitude in my voice.

"No problem. That's my grandson and I can't just sit back and not say anything."

"You know she's gonna be upset that *I* told you," I stressed.

"That should be the least of her concern."

"All right, well, let me know how that conversation goes."

"Trust me, she'll call you before I do."

I chuckled. "Yeah, you got a point there," I told him. "Take care," I added.

"You do the same, buddy," he replied, and then we ended the call.

CHAPTER 6

Ava

While I was reclining on my bed, going through files on Nick's computer, my cell phone rang. I grabbed it from the nightstand and immediately looked at the caller ID and noticed it was my father's number flashing on the screen. Even though I was in the middle of something, seeing his number gave me some comfort, being as though I hadn't spoken to him in about four or five days, so I answered it on the second ring.

"Hello, Dad," I said, sounding warm and cheerful.

"Hi, sweetheart, how are you?" he greeted me back. For some reason his usual jovial demeanor wasn't there.

"I'm good. Are you all right, that's the question," I asked.

"I just got off the phone with Kevin. He told me about what Little Kevin did to his kidnapper."

Hearing my father's words made my heart skip a beat. But somehow, I knew this time would come, the moment when my secret world would collide with the reality I had been so desperately trying to shield my father from. "Look, Dad, I'm sorry you had to find out this way," I replied, my voice faltering slightly.

"Yes, and I'm very disappointed that I had to hear from someone other than my own flesh and blood. But I'm more worried about how you and Little Kevin are holding up," my father said gently. "This must be a lot for you to handle."

I felt a surge of emotions bubbling within me—fear, guilt, anger—all fighting for dominance. "I'm okay, Dad. We're handling it the best way we know how," I assured him, though my own words felt hollow because I really wasn't handling anything. I really just wanted it all to go away.

"So tell me exactly what happened," my father pressed. It was something that I didn't want to talk about, but I knew he wasn't going to let up.

Taken aback by the fact that my father wanted me to go into detail about what happened on the night Little Kevin took Nick's life, I hesitated. I didn't want to think back on that night. I honestly wanted to forget about it and pretend that it never happened. But from the way things were looking tonight, my father wasn't going to allow that to happen.

After carefully choosing my words, I started off saying, "I don't know if Kevin told you or not, but my ex, Nick, was the one who kidnapped the kids—"

"Are you freaking kidding me?" my father blurted out.

"No, I'm not," I assured him. Then I went into grave detail about that awful night, telling my father how I found out Nick was the actual kidnapper, how he attacked me, and then how Little Kevin came to my rescue by picking up the gun I dropped onto the floor and using it to kill Nick.

My father was stunned by my admission. "Baby girl, I really don't know what to say."

"I know it's a lot to take in," I replied.

My father sighed heavily. "Yeah, it is. So, what are you going to do about Little Kevin?"

"What do you mean?"

"Kevin and I both agree that he should get some professional help," my father continued, his tone cautious. "I think it's important for his well-being after such a traumatic event."

My immediate reaction was defensive. "No, Dad," I interjected quickly. "That's not gonna happen. Little Kevin is fine, trust me. Bringing in therapists or counselors will only stir up the hornet's nest. What if they report us? What if he ends up in juvie behind it?"

My father let out another long sigh. He knew I was fiercely protective of my children, but I also wanted him to understand the gravity of this situation. "Ava, honey, I understand your concern. But this isn't something we can just ignore. Do you realize that he committed murder and that this could damage his mental stability?"

"Dad, he's fine," I repeated, trying to convince my father.

"And what makes you say that?"

"Because I know my child. He's still acting the same. He's not having any problems in school. He hasn't been having any nightmares, and to be honest, he doesn't talk about it. Believe me, he's thriving like never before," I explained.

"Well, I still think he needs to receive some professional support because all of that could change one day."

Realizing that my father wasn't letting up, my eyes filled up with unshed tears, and then they started falling from my eyes. "I can't lose him, Dad," I whispered, my voice trembling. "I can't lose my son to the system."

My father's voice softened with empathy. "You won't lose him, Ava. We'll figure this out together. But please consider getting him the help he needs. Because it's not just about avoiding legal consequences; it's about his mental and emotional well-being."

I remained silent for a moment, my mind a whirlwind of conflicting thoughts and fears. But I finally spoke, my voice resigned yet determined. "Okay, Dad, I'll think about it."

My father's relief was palpable through the phone. "Thank you, Ava. I know this isn't easy, but I know you're going to do the right thing," he assured me.

"Believe me, I will," I replied, knowing that I had gotten my father off my back for the moment. At the same time I knew that

I wasn't about to think about anything. My baby boy was not talking to anyone. Not now, not ever. I was keeping him close to the vest and no one else was going to take him from me. Whether anyone knew it or not, my baby was protecting his mother, so I was going to do the same for him at all costs.

My dad and I talked for a few more minutes and then we ended our call. After we hung up, I lay there and thought about what I was going to say to Kevin the next time I spoke to him. It wasn't going to be a cordial conversation, either.

With everything I had going on in my head, I needed to get out of the house on Tuesday morning and get some fresh air. So, once the kids were on the school bus, I decided to get dressed and make a run to Panera Bread and get myself a coffee and breakfast sandwich. The Panera Bread near my home was less than two miles away. It was located in the Armadillo Plaza, along with our local supermarket and a few other restaurants and stores. The landscaping of this entire property was immaculate. It was so inviting.

After I got my food, I took it outside to the outdoor seating area. One table over from me, there were two middle-aged white women eating and sharing small talk. Judging from their conversation, I thought they were soccer moms, one married to an investment banker, while the other to a cosmetic surgeon, and their lives were perfect. I didn't hear a single bad thing about their husbands. In fact, they were praising them for their accomplishments, how their husbands loved them, how they took care of their families, and their philanthropy work in the community.

I had to admit that their lives were on the opposite end of the spectrum from mine. I thought the only people who lived such ideal lives were the people you saw on television, but if everything these ladies were saying was true, then I've witnessed the real thing.

While I listened to their stories of their last vacation in Europe, a tall, handsome Idris Elba look-alike was standing before me. "Excuse me, mind if I join you?" he asked, gesturing to the chair across from me.

I hesitated, but ultimately nodded my head. I mean, how could I tell him no? He gave me the most perfect smile he could muster up. "Thank you," he replied as he took a seat, setting his food down on the table.

"You know you're bold," I commented.

"Why you say that?" he asked.

"Because I could be sitting here waiting on my husband."

"Well, are you?"

"No."

"Are you married?"

"Let's just say that I'm in the middle of a divorce."

"Sorry for his loss!" the guy said. He immediately grabbed the chair, pulled it back, and sat down.

"What's your name?" I asked.

"Neil." He extended his hand, and I extended mine to shake it. His grip was very firm.

"Neil what?"

"Neil Moore. And yours?"

"Ava. Ava Riley," I said, giving him my maiden name, since that's what I'm going back to after my divorce is final.

"Nice name."

"Thank you."

"Do you have kids?"

"Yes, two. Girl and a boy," I said proudly.

"So, where are you from?" His questions continued.

"What makes you think I'm from somewhere else?"

"Because you don't sound like you're from here."

I cracked a smile. "My accent sticks out like a sore thumb, huh?"

"Let's just say that you don't sound like you're from here."

"Well, I'm from Virginia," I told him, realizing when it was too late that I had spoken too soon. I wanted to keep a low profile while I was out here in Houston. I wanted to keep my past back in Virginia, so I could start a new life here in Texas. But it was too late, I'd already given away one important detail about myself. "What about you?" I turned the question back on him.

"I'm originally from LA, but I've had the pleasure of traveling and living in different states for the past twenty years because of the work I used to do."

"What did you used to do?"

"I was an arms dealer . . . for the government."

My eyes widened with surprise as my mind started racing with questions. "Wait, you said you used to be an arms dealer?"

Neil smiled, a hint of amusement in his eyes. "Yes."

"Was it fun?"

"The travel part was fun."

I leaned forward, my gaze intense. "So, why did you leave the government? If you were even employed there at all, Neil."

Neil's smile faded slightly, replaced by a more serious expression. "My work started to get . . . complicated. Too many strings attached, too much bureaucracy. I realized I could be more effective and earn more money on my own terms."

I nodded, understanding the allure of autonomy. "Interesting. So, what do you do now?"

"I still do it, but I operate privately, on the side. It's more like consulting than anything else. But I have a few clients who call me from time to time and under very strict conditions," he explained, his voice low and measured.

I took a moment to digest the information. "Out of curiosity, how did you get into that line of work?"

Neil's smile widened. "Long story short . . . I started in the military, then I transitioned into intelligence. One thing led to another, and I found myself in the arms trade. It's a world of shadows and secrets, but it pays well if you know what you're doing," he explained.

Intrigued by his status, I sat up in the chair and said, "So the clients that you have now, are they like gun enthusiasts, Mafia types, or terrorists?"

Apparently amused by my question, he chuckled. "No, no, no . . . I only deal with enthusiasts. And actually, the work I do now is more about connections and less about the actual arms. Information is just as valuable as any weapon," he replied, his eyes watching me carefully.

I shifted in my seat, considering his words. "Good to know."

"So, what do you do?" he asked.

"Well, I'm a stay-at-home mother now. Going through a divorce, like I mentioned before, so I get a salary from the family business."

"And what is that?"

"Auto parts dealer. Not as exotic as an arms dealer, though."

"Storefronts?"

"Yes, we have a couple of them back on the East Coast."

"Nice. So, how long have you been in Houston?"

"A few months now," I answered.

"Like it?"

"It's a change that I can get used to."

"So, how far do you live from here?"

"Not far," I said, refusing to give him the exact location of my residence. "And you?"

"I'm about five miles away. I live in a town house near Post Oak."

"I'm sorry, I don't know where that is."

"It's a really nice area. Been there for a year and a half now."

"Cool. So, what do you do for fun?" I wanted to know.

"I like to hang out at the sports bar. Maybe go on a fishing trip. And I'll do a little camping every now and again."

"Sounds pretty adventurous."

"What about you?"

"I don't have any hobbies outside of my kids. My life is pretty much centered around them; so whatever they want to do, we do it."

"Well, we might have to get together one day and change all of that," he said confidently.

"We shall see," I stated, not looking too much into his comment. Where I stood with my kids was, they already had a father and didn't need another. With the kidnapping incident still fresh in my mind, no other man was going to come within twenty feet of them for a while. Nick was someone I trusted—and he proved to be just the opposite.

Neil and I talked until I finished my breakfast, and right before I made my exit, he asked me for my phone number. I didn't give him mine, but I took his and promised him that I'd use it soon. He accepted that answer and then we parted ways.

On the way home I had to admit it was nice having a conversation with someone other than Paulina and my soon-to-be ex-husband. It was also kind of refreshing being in the presence of that man. He was so big, tall, and handsome. I had to admit that he was definitely the type of man I would date. But dating someone now was absolutely out of the question. My main focus was my children, and it will remain that way for some time now. Maybe if he sticks around for a while, we could see what happens.

CHAPTER 7

Lacey

IT HAD BEEN TWO DAYS SINCE I WIRED KEVIN THE THIRTY GRAND I promised him, but he had yet to give me Ava's home address in Houston, so I got him on the line. He didn't hesitate to answer my call.

"Hello," he said.

"I wired you the money on Monday, but you never got back to me with Ava's address," I reminded him.

"Oh, shit! My bad, Lacey. I've been meaning to do that."

"I thought you ran off with my money," I joked.

I heard a shuffling sound in the background. "I've got it right here," he assured me.

"All right, let me get something to write with," I replied, and grabbed a pen I saw lying on the desk in Maceo's office. "Okay, go ahead."

"It's 555 Acorn Avenue, Houston, Texas," he replied.

As quickly as he read it off to me, I wrote it down on the desk-size calendar that was on my husband's desk. "Okay, got it," I stated.

"Sorry about that," he apologized again.

"It's all good."

"So, when are you guys heading that way?" he asked.

My first thought was to withhold that information, but then I remembered Maceo and I planned to kill him after we murdered his wife, so I told him. "In four days."

"You mean, you're going out there on Sunday?"

"Yes."

"And that's the day you're gonna do the job?" He wanted clarity.

"Yes."

"Are you going to take her away from the house? Or are you going to do it there? Because remember, I don't want my kids nowhere around."

"You said you're gonna fly out there and get them, right?" I jogged his memory.

"Yeah, I'm gonna fly out there before your arrival," he declared.

"Okay, cool. Then it's settled. But remember, you cannot let her know what's coming her way. If this whole thing blows up in our faces, *you* will suffer the consequences for it," I threatened.

"Oh no! You have my word. I won't say anything to her. All I care about is my kids' safety. That's it. I don't care what you do to her. But let me say this, she has a nanny named Paulina, who lives at the house with her, too."

"Glad you mentioned that. So, how old is this nanny?"

"She's an older woman. She'll be really easy."

"Good to know," I commented. But realistically, I didn't need for Kevin to tell me how things were going to be. My team and I were experts at this shit. Kevin doesn't know the first thing about killing anyone, because to my knowledge, he has never done it. What I need him to do is keep his mouth closed until I need him to answer a question for me. "Well, look, I'm gonna go for now. But if I need anything else, I'll hit you up."

"Okay, cool."

"All right, you take care."

"You do the same."

CHAPTER 8

Kevin

"WHO WAS THAT YOU WERE TALKING TO?" TY ASKED AFTER walking up behind me. I swear, it seemed like she came out of nowhere.

I changed the subject. "I thought you were out on your morning run?"

"I was, but I came back early. Now tell me, who were you just talking to?" she pressed.

Reluctant to answer her, I stalled by asking her another question. "Why were you eavesdropping on my conversation?"

"Kevin, you're deflecting," she made it a point to say.

"No, I'm not."

"Well, then, tell me who were you talking to?" She pressured me to answer. I knew then that she wasn't going to let up.

I sat there as anxiety and dread consumed me. I knew I couldn't tell Ty who I had been speaking to—and about what—because she'd look at me as a monster and probably wouldn't understand.

"Well, since you don't wanna reveal who you were talking to, then at least tell me if that conversation had anything to do with your wife?"

"What makes you say that?"

"Because you told the mysterious person that you didn't want your kids around when this thing went down. You also said something about flying somewhere out of town so you can get in and out before their arrival."

I sat there dumbfounded. I had nothing to say. I had been caught red-handed, and trying to talk my way out of this mess was going to be extremely hard to do.

"So you're just gonna sit there and ignore me?"

I could tell she was losing patience with me. "What do you want me to say?" I finally answered.

"I want you to tell me what's going on."

"I wish I could, Ty, but I can't. The less you know, the better off you'll be."

"Did you put a target on your wife's back?" she asked. Her facial expression had turned sour.

"Do you want me to lie to you?"

"Of course not."

"Well, I'm sorry, but I can't say. Like I just said, it's best that you don't know anything."

"Kevin, I don't want to hear that crap!" she roared. "Now, if you don't tell me what's going on, I am going to take your phone and call that person back. I'll make them tell me what y'all talked about."

"No, you will not," I said adamantly, and slid my cell phone into my pocket.

Ty stormed toward me and held her hand out. "Give me your phone right now!" she demanded.

I refused to waver. "I'm sorry, but I can't."

"So you're not gonna give me your phone?" she asked once again.

"I wish I could, Ty. But I can't."

With an expression of disappointment and defeat, Ty huffed and said, "You're gonna regret this." Then she stormed off like a bat out of hell.

I had no idea what she meant by that comment, but at this point I couldn't put too much thought into it. I had bigger fish to fry and figured that in a few days she'd forget all about it and we'd be right back where we were before she overheard my conversation.

After she left the room, I pulled my cell phone back out of my pocket and logged onto the Delta website and booked myself a flight out to Houston for Friday. I figured going out there two days before Lacey and her crew were due to arrive would be more than enough time to meet up with Ava, pick up my kids, and get them away from the destruction that was about to come. I was sure that my kids were going to be excited about seeing me, and when I tell them we're going to spend the entire weekend together, they're gonna jump for joy. All I needed to do now was book a room and my trip will be finalized.

Once I went through the list of hotels in downtown Houston, I decided to stay at the Lancaster Hotel and paid for it, since it was close to everything, including the Houston Zoo and Minute Maid Park. I figured these two places would be on the bucket list of places that the kids would want to visit when I got there.

After I received my confirmation number, I closed the browser on my cell phone and smiled at the thought of seeing my kids in a couple of days after four long months of not having them around. I had the urge to text Ava to tell her I would be coming their way on Friday, but then I decided against it. The way she'd been acting lately, it wouldn't surprise me if she tried to derail my trip by taking the kids away from the house and pulling a disappearing act before I got there.

Now, that would really screw up my plans, and Lacey's too, and I can't have that. So I figured it would be best to leave well enough alone. I looked at the photo of my kids on my phone's screen saver and mumbled quietly, "See you guys in a couple of days," and then I slid my phone back into my pants pocket.

CHAPTER 9

Lacey & Maceo

"WHAT ARE YOU DOING?" MACEO ASKED AFTER HE ENTERED his office in the garage and saw me sitting behind his desk, my fingers rhythmically hitting the keyboard as I looked at the computer screen.

"Looking at the house this bitch purchased with my brother's money," I replied. My facial expression darkened as I stared at the house, my mind racing at the thought of getting revenge.

Maceo walked over and glanced at the computer screen; his expression changed, too, as he took in the sight of the lavish house. "What's that, the satellite view?" he wondered aloud as I used the mouse to zoom in on every corner of the home.

"Yes," I answered him as he stood beside me, his arms crossed tightly over his chest.

"Wow! So this is where she's been hiding," he muttered, his eyes narrowing as he studied the image on the screen.

"Yeah, and the bitch used my brother's money to buy this fucking house, too. This bitch had the nerve to kill my blood and then live off the money that he earned from his blood, sweat, and tears. But that's all gonna end this weekend, so she better enjoy what she can while she can."

Maceo's gaze hardened as he continued to look at the screen. "Yeah, she better enjoy it now."

Upon hearing Maceo's words, I turned to face him. His eyes were burning with intensity. "I want to fly to Houston this Saturday, so I need you to call the hit man. Tell him I want her gone *before* eleven fifty-nine on Sunday night. Not on Monday or Tuesday. A minute before midnight, on Sunday night, at the latest," I instructed him.

Maceo nodded, pulling out his phone and dialing a number from memory. The room fell silent as he spoke in hushed tones, arranging the final details of the plan.

While he was talking to the hit man, my thoughts drifted back to memories of my brother and his laughter instantly echoed in my mind. Nick was a good man. He was also a good brother to me. We were very close, and if I needed anything, he'd stop whatever he was doing to take care of my needs. No questions asked. He was a solid guy—a soldier to the bone.

I clenched my fists, feeling the weight of betrayal and loss. "Oh yeah, let him know that Ava has a nanny living with her and I want her gone, too. I don't want any witnesses left behind," I blurted out while Maceo was giving instructions to our hit man.

He nodded, and his expression hardened because he understood the gravity of the situation.

The call with our guy lasted for about three minutes longer; then Maceo put his phone away. "It's done. He's gonna meet us in Houston on Saturday," Maceo informed me.

"Good," I said, rubbing my hands together as my frown turned into a smile. Out of nowhere a sense of satisfaction filled the room. The thought of seeing this bitch beg for her life as she took her final breath was all the revenge I needed; in just a couple of days, I will get just that.

A few minutes later, Maceo and I heard a knock on his office door. We both looked at the door.

"Who is it?" he asked.

"It's Jake, boss. We've got a delivery."

"Okay, I'll be right out," Maceo told him, and then he turned his attention toward me. "Let me go handle this and I'll be right back."

"I'll be right here," I assured him.

Immediately after Maceo walked away from me, I turned my attention back to the computer screen. My mind seemed to already be in motion about how I wanted my crew and me to enter the house and the ways I wanted her tortured. I even thought about what I was going to say to that bitch when I saw her.

Believe me, she will feel my wrath before taking her last breath.

CHAPTER 10

Ty

I DON'T KNOW IF KEVIN NOTICED IT WHILE WE WERE IN BED THE night before, but I tossed and turned all night long after listening to the tail end of his conversation just hours before I lay down. He did his best to pretend like nothing happened by fixing dinner, cracking jokes about how he looked in his pajamas, and putting Annabelle to sleep when it was my night to do it. As much as I wanted to bring the subject back up, I left well enough alone.

When I woke up this morning, I got the urge to bring up that phone conversation again, but I knew he was going to give me some pushback. Instead, I decided to not say anything about it at all. But that didn't change the fact I needed to talk to someone about it. Shortly after Kevin left the house to attend a meeting with an auto parts wholesale distributor, which was located about forty-five minutes from our house, I got on the phone and called Whitney. She was the only person I could trust with this information.

While the phone rang, my mind started swirling with a mix of confusion and worry as I thought back on the bits and pieces of the conversation I heard coming from Kevin's mouth. I had to admit that the conversation between him and that unknown person about his wife, Ava, had stunned me. I tried to dismiss the whole thing after I walked away from him last night, but the more I thought about it, the more certain I became that something awful was about to happen.

The phone rang twice before Whitney answered. Her voice was as warm as usual. "Hey, girl! Good morning!"

"Whitney, I need to talk to you about something serious," I said, my voice betraying my unease.

"What's wrong?" Sensing my distress, Whitney shifted her tone instantly.

I took a deep breath and exhaled. "Last night I overheard Kevin talking to someone about Ava. And I think he was saying something about getting rid of her and the nanny," I explained.

There was a sharp intake of breath from Whitney's end. "Wait, what? Are you sure you heard right?" Whitney said with disbelief.

"Listen, I was coming in from running and I walked inside the house and overheard him asking the person on the other end of the phone if they were planning on taking Ava away from her house because he doesn't want his kids around. Then on top of that, he also warned the caller that she had a nanny who was up there in age, so she'd be easy to get rid of, too," I added.

"Wait, are you sure you heard that?"

"Yes, Whitney, I'm sure," I replied, my voice tinged with fear.

"Does he know you heard him?"

"Yes, right after he hung up with the person, I asked him point-blank who he was talking to, and he refused to tell me. The only answer he gave me was that it was best I didn't know."

"No fucking way!"

"Yes, girl . . ." I paused and then said, "I think Kevin might have put out a hit on Ava and the nanny."

Whitney was silent for a moment, processing the gravity of my words. "Oh, my God, Ty. That's . . . that's really serious. What are you going to do about it?"

I shook my head, even though Whitney couldn't see me. "I don't know, that's why I called you. Shit, I was hoping you'd tell me I was hearing things, that it's all in my mind, or maybe it's all just a misunderstanding."

"Hell nah! If I were there and heard that same conversation, I would've come to the same conclusion."

"So, what should I do?"

"Ty, all I'm gonna say is, trust your intuitions. If you feel something wasn't right about the conversation Kevin had with that person, then nine times out of ten, you're right."

"You're still not telling me what I should do about it."

"Have you thought about talking to Ava?"

I sighed. "I considered it, but I don't know how she'll react. Plus, if Kevin really is planning to have someone hurt her, I don't want to blow the whistle on Kevin by tipping her off."

"But what if he's trying to have her killed? And you find out later that you could've prevented her death?"

"I thought about that," I admitted.

"So, then, maybe you should talk to the authorities anonymously. They can investigate without anyone knowing it was you who reported it."

I sat there quietly, considering Whitney's suggestion. "You know what, that might be my best option. But then again, what if the cops find out who I am and rat me out? Kevin would never forgive me because he'll feel betrayed. That alone could end our relationship. And then I'll be just another single mother walking around with a brand-new baby."

"Well, just let whatever happens, happen."

I let out a long sigh. "I don't know . . ."

"Well, you may not know now, but you sure have a lot to think about."

"Don't remind me."

"Other than that, how are you feeling?" Whitney asked.

"To be perfectly honest, I really don't know how to feel, especially after the conversation I heard Kevin have. It's like when he and Ava separated, and he came here to live full-time with me and the baby, I thought things would be great. Instead, it's like the more we're together, the more I see the real him. And I don't like it."

"What do you mean?"

"Well, I never told you this, but these last couple of weeks, he's been acting really strange. He'll walk outside or drive away from the house to make calls. Sometimes he'll tell me he's going to one place, and I'll check his location and he's somewhere else. Not only that, but he's also been really secretive about stuff lately, too. It's crazy. It's almost like he's a different person."

"Oh, wow! That's not good."

"I know. And you know I can't deal with a person who's secretive and lies."

"Yes, I know. But do you think it's another woman?"

"I don't know. But everything he's doing in the dark will eventually come to light."

"Yeah, you got that right," Whitney agreed.

Whitney and I talked for a few more minutes until she got a call from her man, Todd, and then she had to hang up. She did assure me she'd call back later to check on me. And before she hung up, I thanked her for listening.

As far as what I was going to do about this situation, I didn't have the slightest clue, but I will figure it out sooner rather than later.

Kevin came home a few hours later acting like he had just struck gold. His spirits were soaring high. I knew that it probably had something to do with that business meeting he went to earlier, so I waited for him to tell me the good news as he kicked off his shoes at the doorway.

I was sitting on the sofa, watching television, when he walked into the living room. As soon as we locked eyes, he instantly knew there was a lingering displeasure from the previous night's disagreement. His mood immediately changed the moment he realized the tension between us had not dissipated.

"Guess what, babe? I nailed that deal with the auto parts distributor today. We're looking at a solid partnership that could boost our sales by at least seventy percent!" he cheerfully exclaimed, trying to lighten the mood.

I forced a smile, acknowledging his achievement, but I failed miserably at masking my inner turmoil. "That's nice," I replied nonchalantly, pretending to be preoccupied with what was on TV.

Kevin sensed my dismissive behavior, but decided to push through anyway by elaborating on the details of the deal and highlighting the potential benefits for our future together. "Do you know what this would do for us?" he asked me, trying to get me to engage with him.

"I'm sure it will do a lot," I finally said, still focusing on the television movie that was playing.

"Ty, it would do more than a lot. This deal would set us up for the rest of our lives."

"That's nice," I added, my voice flat.

"What's wrong with you?" he asked, taking a seat next to me.

I turned my head slightly so we could be face-to-face. "Do you even have to ask?" I replied sarcastically.

"Don't tell me you're still upset about last night," he shot back.

"Duh!"

"Come on now, Ty, why you gotta bring that back up? I'm trying to have a good day and express the joy and happiness I've got going on, and you wanna bring up old stuff."

"Because it's *not* old. And it needs to be addressed."

"Look, we're not going to do this right now. I just got the best news of my career, and you want to ruin it by bringing up something that happened yesterday—and it doesn't even concern you in the first place," Kevin stated.

I could tell that he was irritated. I raised my eyebrows with discontent. I mean, how dare he make a comment like that to me? "It may not have anything to do with me directly, but it had something to do with your wife. And I didn't like what I heard." I made my displeasure known to him.

"Look, just mind your business, Ty. Like I said last night, the less you know, the better off you'll be," he responded harshly.

"So, what is that advice?" I spat, and my face folded into a frown. I was feeling heated now more than ever. But before Kevin could come back with a rebuttal, the faint cry of our baby echoed from the nursery.

Kevin turned his attention in that direction, and before I could volunteer to go and get her, he beat me to the punch. "Guess nap time is over," he said, giving off a sense of relief, jumping up from the sofa. Seconds later, he raced out of the living room and didn't look back.

But I refused to let him off the hook. We were going to finish this conversation, so I followed him into Annabelle's nursery. When I entered the room, he was holding her in his arms, filling her face up with one kiss after the other. He was very happy to see her. "Are you Daddy's girl?" he asked her, trying to avoid eye contact with me.

"Are you sending someone to kill your wife?" I blurted out.

Kevin shot me a sharp look. I could tell that he was both appalled and disturbed by my question, but he remained mum.

So I pressed him. "Answer my question, Kevin. Are you trying to get rid of your wife and the nanny?"

He chuckled nervously. "Where did you get that ridiculous idea from?"

"I heard your conversation. You asked the person if they were taking Ava away from the house or were they keeping her there. And then at the end, you told the person she had a nanny living with her, but she would be easy. So, tell me, what does all of this mean?" I asked calmly.

Kevin's face was instantly riddled with guilt, and I could tell he was at a loss for words after giving me an odd stare. I thought at one point he was going to clear things up for me, but he didn't. Instead, he brushed me off.

"Not right now, and especially not around her," he said in a dismissive manner. Then he turned his focus back on the baby and started talking to her again. "You love your daddy, Annabelle?" He smiled cheerfully.

Angry from the way he'd just dismissed me, I turned around and stormed out of the room.

CHAPTER 11

Ava

IT WAS FRIDAY MORNING AND PAULINA AND I WERE IN THE MIDDLE OF grocery shopping at H-E-B when I received a phone call from my kids' school principal, Yvette Lucas. I put her on hold, handed Paulina the grocery list, instructed her to pick up the rest of the things we needed and to meet me at the self-checkout line when she was done. After she said okay, I got back to my call.

"I'm sorry about that," I told the principal.

"Oh, no problem," she replied.

"How can I help you?" I asked.

"I'm sorry to bother you, Mrs. Frost, but something disturbing happened during recess today involving your son and another little boy," the school principal started off.

My stomach tightened instantly. "What happened?"

"From what I'm told, your son, Kevin, started bullying a classmate of his. Apparently, the other boy said something to your son that he didn't like. At that point the situation escalated, and Kevin threatened to bring a gun to school and shoot him with it. The other boy's reply was 'No, you won't.' And Kevin's reply was 'Yes, I will, because I've done it before,' " Mrs. Lucas explained, her tone heavy with the weight of the words.

At that very moment I swallowed a lump of fear and anxiety, and it sat in the pit of my stomach. "Are you sure? Because Little Kevin would never say something like that," I answered, brusquely asking for clarification.

"Trust me, I understand your disbelief, Mrs. Frost. However, several children in his class also heard the threat," she reported, her words full of regret.

"Where is he now?" I wanted to know. My face was red-hot with fury as my thoughts started swirling. How could he have done this? What was on his mind? Was this stemming from the shooting incident involving Nick? And was this going to be the start of a mental health issue that will affect him long-term?

"I have him here in the office with me right now. Want to speak with him?"

"Absolutely," I said with certainty, but not knowing what I really wanted to say to him, especially while he was standing in front of his principal. I didn't want to put my baby boy in a compromising situation by asking him awkward questions around her, so I decided to keep things to a minimum.

"Okay, here he is," she announced.

There was a brief pause, and then a few seconds later, I heard Little Kevin's voice tinged with fear. "Hello?" I could tell that he was scared.

"Little Kevin, honey, what's going on?" I asked, choosing my words carefully.

"Mom, he started it first," Little Kevin replied, his words slightly shaky.

"What happened?" I continued.

"He was bullying Kamryn on the bus this morning and I told him to leave her alone."

"Did he?"

"Yes, but when we went out to the playground, he got with his friends and they started bullying me." He got defensive as he started explaining.

"Calm down, baby! It'll be all right. So, listen, I'm gonna end this conversation for now, but when you get home, we'll finish it, okay?" I said softly. I didn't want to cause a scare or have him shut down on me.

"Okay."

"Oh yeah, and you may get suspended for this, but don't worry about it. We'll deal with this whole thing together, okay?"

"Okay."

"All right. Well, put Mrs. Lucas back on the phone, and I'll see you later."

"Okay," he said, and then there was a short pause.

"Mrs. Frost, I'm back," Mrs. Lucas announced.

"All right. So, what's going to happen now?" I got straight to the point.

"Well, since we have a strict school policy on bullying, and especially if a child threatens to bring a gun to school, we are bound by that policy to suspend him for ten days."

"Ten days!" I shouted, garnering stares from nearby store patrons.

"Yes, ma'am. Now, I could've given him twenty-one days, because he threatened the child with a gun and bragged that he has killed someone before—"

"Well, that's not true," I interjected.

"I didn't believe that myself when I heard the children tell me, but nevertheless, he did threaten the child by saying that he would bring a firearm to school—"

"I don't know where he would get one from. My husband and I are separated, and I don't own a gun," I cut her off again.

"Well, again, that's neither here nor there. The fact remains, he threatened the child, so we have to abide by our school's policy. Now you may request a hearing in front of our school board members, but that could be an epic failure. That's not to say, I wouldn't try if you think my sanction is too harsh."

"No, that won't be necessary," I said, because at this point I just wanted to get my son and bring him home before this whole thing got more out of hand than it already had. "But I have a question," I added.

"Sure, what is it?"

"What's going to happen to the little boy who bullied my daughter on the bus?"

"Nothing, since your daughter hasn't reported it."

"What if she does?"

"Well, then, we'll conduct an investigation, like we did with your son. Then we'll take the appropriate measures to correct the situation."

"So, will he get suspended, too?"

"I can't say right now."

"How convenient," I commented sarcastically.

"Well, is that it?" the principal asked, sounding as if she was concluding the conversation.

"Yeah," I responded nonchalantly.

"Okay, well, I'm gonna get my secretary to type up his suspension notice, and it will be put in the mail tomorrow. But as for right now, I'm gonna need someone to come and pick him up from school."

Taken aback by her swift action to get him off school grounds, I asked, "So he's not allowed to take the bus home?"

"No, I'm afraid not. Someone has to come and get him within the hour."

I screamed silently in my head as my cheeks turned red and my nostrils flared. But somehow, I held my composure and said, "Okay, I will be there within the hour."

"Great, he'll be waiting in the main office," she stated.

"I'm sure he will," I said, my words barely audible.

"I'm sorry, did you say something?" she asked me.

"I said thank you," I lied, and then I disconnected the call.

Immediately after I paid for the groceries, Paulina and I put the bags inside the car and climbed in. During the drive I told Paulina I had received a call from the kids' school principal and told her everything Mrs. Lucas said, even the part where Little Kevin was getting suspended for ten days.

Paulina sat in the passenger seat, shocked. "Did you get a chance to speak with Little Kevin?"

"Yes, I spoke with him briefly," I acknowledged.

"So, what did he say?" She seemed concerned.

"Little Kevin admitted to doing what she said he had done. But he also told me that the same boy had bullied Kamryn on the bus this morning on the way to school, which was why he said what he said to him," I explained.

"So, what's gonna happen to the little boy who bullied Kamryn on the bus?" Paulina wanted to know.

"Mrs. Lucas gave me some bogus spiel about how Kamryn needs to report the incident and then they'll go through the investigation phase after that."

"So, will the kid get suspended, too?"

"She said that she couldn't say right now, which means he's not."

Paulina let out a long sigh. "You're probably right," she said. "I wonder what made Little Kevin say that he would bring a gun to school?" Paulina inquired. She was curious to know. But I couldn't tell her the real reason why he said that, because she wouldn't understand. I also refuse to put her in a predicament where she would look at my son differently.

I tried my best to keep Little Kevin from telling anyone about what he did to save my life from Nick, but that all went out the window when he told his father. And then, what do you know, Big Kevin told my father, so now two people outside of me and Little Kevin know what happened. No one else can find out. Now, as far as how I'm going to handle things with Little Kevin, I can't say, because I'm still grappling with the whole incident, in and of itself. I do know that he and I will have a serious talk, since this can't ever happen again.

"I'm sure he said it just to scare the boy, because you and I both know he does not have access to a gun, because I sure as hell don't have one," I pointed out.

Paulina nodded her head in agreement.

She and I talked more about the situation until I arrived at the school. It was approximately eleven-fifteen in the morning when I walked into the main office. When I asked to speak with Mrs. Lucas, I was told that she was in a meeting with another parent, so I signed Little Kevin out. Then I requested the office secretary to call and have Kamryn's teacher release her from class, too, because I was signing her out and taking her home as well.

She was so happy to see me. More shocked than anything that she was leaving school early. "Why me and Little Kevin leaving school so early, Mommy?" her little voice asked.

"I'll explain it to you later, baby," I told her, and then we all exited the school.

Back in the car, the kids spoke to Paulina and then everyone rode back home listening to Paulina's Spanish-music playlist. The kids used to complain about it, but since the kidnapping, they haven't griped about it one bit.

The moment we arrived home, we all pitched in and took the groceries inside the house. Kamryn volunteered to help Paulina put the food away. "Keep her occupied while I talk to Little Kevin in his bedroom," I instructed Paulina. After she gave me a nod, Little Kevin and I headed to his bedroom.

Once inside, he and I took a seat on his bed and I broke the ice by saying, "How are you feeling right now?"

He hunched his shoulders and replied, "I don't know."

"Do you think I'm upset with you?"

"Maybe," he said.

I grabbed his right hand and held it between both of mine and instructed him to look into my eyes. After he had done so, I said, "Listen, honey, in no way am I upset that you got suspended from school, because at the end of the day, you stood up for your sister. But what I am concerned about is the part where you told the little boy that you'll bring a gun to school and kill him with it because you've done it before."

Little Kevin dropped his head. So I used one of my hands to lift his chin and his head back up. "Look at me when I'm talking to you. This is serious."

He looked back at me and gave me a disappointing glare. This broke my heart. "Baby, you can't say things like that, and especially to kids at school. You see how those kids ran to the teacher and got you in trouble?"

Little Kevin shifted uncomfortably. "Mom, I was just trying to protect Kamryn. They were picking on her, and I wasn't going to have it!" he stated boldly.

Proud of his protective nature, I nodded, acknowledging the fact that he defended his sister when she needed him. "Look, I told you I'm not upset that you stood up for your sister, but threatening to take a gun to school is not the way to handle things. Then on top of that, you bragged to the kid about killing someone. Baby, I know you thought that by saying that, it would scare him, but look at how he ratted you out. What if the principal would've believed that you killed someone and called CPS to come and investigate? Do you know there's a chance that you and your sister could be taken from me?"

Little Kevin's facial expression turned sheepish. "I'm sorry,

Ma, I didn't know. But he just made me so mad and that was the first thing I thought of saying."

I sighed and placed my hand around his shoulder. "Okay, I'm with you, but you have to think before you act, especially when it comes to something as serious as bringing a weapon to school and telling people that you've killed someone. Got it?" I said, sounding gentle but firm.

Little Kevin nodded, understanding the gravity of his actions. "Got it," he said earnestly.

"Good," I said, acknowledging that I appreciated his willingness to admit his mistake. "Because that's not something to be proud of," I added.

"But I was proud of that. Dad's friend was trying to kill you, and if I hadn't grabbed that gun and shot him, then we'd probably all be dead."

My mouth sagged on each side while my heart thundered at my son's response. I immediately thought: *What has happened to my little boy? Has he turned into an unremorseful killer? Was Kevin right? Will we really have to get him some psychological help? What would the therapist do or say after he or she hears my son's admission?*

After thinking about the bad things that would follow, I dismissed the whole idea and tried to look at things from my son's perspective. He said he was proud of the fact that he protected me—then that's what it is.

"Baby, believe me, I am totally grateful for what you did. But that doesn't mean that you get to go around telling people about it. We don't need no one coming around here investigating us, okay?"

Little Kevin sucked his teeth, as if getting a little aggravated with me. "Mom, I know already."

"All right, so let today be a lesson and now we're gonna move on from it. Deal?"

"Deal."

I hugged my son tightly, feeling relieved that we had the talk, but concerned this situation may turn into something else.

As Little Kevin was about to stand up, I grabbed his arm and said, "Don't tell your dad that you got suspended. He's not gonna understand, like I did."

"Okay, I won't," he promised.

CHAPTER 12

Kevin

TY AND I HAVEN'T BEEN TALKING THESE PAST COUPLE OF DAYS. SHE'S even slept in our daughter's nursery to avoid being around me. Whether she knows it or not, her hiding out has helped me get out of telling her that I am flying to Houston to see my kids tomorrow morning. I was even able to pack a few things in my business briefcase, so she won't question me when I leave.

Tonight, after she put the baby to bed and lay down beside her, I tried to get the kids on the phone, but Ava, of course, didn't answer her cell phone. I was disappointed, to say the least. But I figured all I have to endure is one more day and I will finally be able to see and talk to them without her permission. And then after this hit goes down in three days, I will have them permanently and I'll be a million dollars richer. Now, what more can a man ask for? Nothing.

On Friday morning I rose at six forty-five, because my flight was scheduled to leave the Richmond Airport at ten thirty-two. On my way out of the house, I planned to tell Ty that I had to drive to the Tidewater area to check on things with my other store. I know she'd believe me, because I've never lied to her before.

So, as I showered and got dressed, she came strolling into the room with the baby in her arms. When she saw me fully dressed, she asked where was I going?

"I've gotta run down and check on my store. Then I'm gonna stop at my old house to see if anything's out of place," I replied.

"Why didn't you tell me that last night? You normally tell me days in advance when you're going out of town," she pointed out.

"I was going to tell you this morning. I would've told you sooner if you hadn't been avoiding me like the plague," I lied.

"That's not an excuse, Kevin. I don't like it when you keep things from me."

"I don't keep things away from you."

"You still haven't told me who you were talking to on the phone the other night, or why you said what you said to them," she reminded me.

I huffed. "Okay, I've gotta go," I said, grabbing my briefcase. I kissed her and my little girl on their foreheads and then walked out of our bedroom.

"There you go, running away again. You're becoming really good at that." She raised her voice just enough so that I would hear her, but not so much that it would scare the baby.

I ignored her and continued out of the house. I wasn't going to allow her to make me miss my flight to Houston. Not today. As I drove away from the house, I noticed her looking out the living-room window. I could tell she was extremely upset with me, and I was going to catch her wrath when she eventually found out that I lied to her and that I was really in Houston. Shit will definitely hit the fan. But I figured she'd eventually get over it.

Right now, I had major issues to handle, and getting my children out of harm's way before Lacey and Maceo arrived in

Houston was more important than an argument I would be facing when I returned home.

The flight to Houston was only two and a half hours and I slept through the entire thing, so it seemed like it took no time to arrive in the Bayou City. I had the urge to call Ava to let her know that I was in town to get the kids, but then I figured I would rather see the look on her face when she opened her front door and saw me standing on her doorstep. Yeah, that would be fun. After I made my way through the terminal, I headed down to ground transportation, where I picked up my rental car. From there, I typed Ava's home address into the car's GPS system, and as soon as it registered, I saw it was only twenty-seven minutes away. I put the car in drive and headed to Ava's house.

I have to admit that when I drove through Ava's upscale community, I was astonished at the two-story rustic homes built in this neighborhood. Every lawn was well-manicured, accompanied by long driveways. Ava's brick home, built with stone veneer, sat perched atop a hill, with at least three acres of land surrounding it. I couldn't believe how she had leveled up. This property made our home in Virginia look like a starter home. Nick's money and mine had definitely changed her life for sure. I also had to admit that my once-undying love for Ava had withered into contempt and resentment. Here she was in Houston living the good life with my money and Nick's, while I'm back in Virginia getting favors from Lacey and making deals with auto parts distributors just to keep my business afloat.

But after this weekend, I will get back what rightfully belonged to me. And as for my part of the ransom, I'll be getting my kids back. As soon as Lacey kills the bitch, I will have an extra $1,000,000 in cash. Not to mention, I will get all the proceeds from the house when it's sold, and I'll claim the life insurance policy for Ava's death. Yeah, I'm about to become a rich man—and no one is going to stop it.

As I approached her home, I decided to drive up the spiral driveway. I cruised up on her property slowly, wondering if she was home. I could see from afar she had a Ring cam. I even noticed she had surveillance cameras mounted up on both sides of the house, too. I can't say if she had them placed there for the kids' protection or hers because she robbed a man who was related to some very dangerous people, and she needed to make sure no one was watching her home. So I say, clever girl, but she's gonna need more than security cameras to get Lacey and her men out of her house. Those people are ruthless, and when they set out to kill someone, they will accomplish that mission.

I finally stopped and parked the car about ten feet away from the garage door. Immediately after I climbed out of the car, I closed the door behind me and inhaled the fresh scent of Ava's newly cut grass. Her massive landscape was beautiful, to say the least, and once again the feeling of resentment and jealousy consumed me for a second. But I shook it off because I was on a mission to recoup Little Kevin and Kamryn. I walked up to the front door and rang the doorbell.

"Mommy, someone is at the door," I heard my daughter shout from inside the house. This made my heart jump for joy. But I also wondered why she was at home this time of the day. Wasn't she supposed to be in school?

Seconds later, the door opened, and Paulina appeared in the doorway. I could immediately tell that she was surprised to see me, but she played it off and flashed a fake smile. "Mr. Frost, it's nice to see you," she said.

"Nice to see you as well," I replied.

"I'm sorry, but is Mrs. Frost expecting you? Because she didn't mention anything to me about you coming."

"No, she's not expecting me. I flew out here to surprise my

children, since I haven't seen them in over four months," I told her.

"Daddy!" my daughter shouted as she appeared at the front door and shot outside to hug me. Her actions melted my heart. I dropped my briefcase and picked her up off her feet and scooped her into the air. "Hi, baby!" I greeted her as I filled her face with kisses.

"You coming to get us?" she wondered aloud.

Before I could answer her, Ava also appeared at the front door, alongside Paulina. "What are you doing here?" she asked petulantly, her voice low, almost a growl. She eyed me evilly as her nostrils moved in and out as she stood there with folded arms.

"I wanted to surprise my kids," I responded, mustering up the biggest smile I could. I wasn't about to let her rain on my parade, or get into a confrontation with her in front of my daughter. I was there to get my kids and there was nothing she could do about it at this point.

"You should've called first," she continued as she looked over at my rental car and then turned her attention back toward me.

"I did. I called several times, but you didn't answer."

"What's up, Dad?" Little Kevin shouted as he, too, appeared at the front door and shot past his mother and embraced me around my waist with a bear hug.

"Hey, son!" I said with excitement.

"Are you taking us somewhere, Dad?" Little Kevin wanted to know.

"Yeah, Daddy, can we go somewhere?" Kamryn chimed in.

"Absolutely," I answered, looking at both of them dead in the eyes, avoiding the hard stare Ava was giving me. I could feel the heat coming off her from where I was standing.

"Kevin, you just can't pop up in town and make plans with the kids without consulting me first. How do you know I didn't already have something planned?" she interjected.

"Mom, you don't have anything planned for us," Little Kevin blurted out.

"Be quiet! You don't know what I could've been planning behind the scenes," Ava added.

"Well, do you?" I finally turned my attention back toward her.

"No, but I could've is all I'm saying," she rebutted.

"Yay! We can go with Daddy! We can go with Daddy!" Kamryn shouted for joy.

"So, where are we going, Dad?" Little Kevin asked.

"Have you guys been to the zoo or the museum?" I asked them.

"We've been to the zoo, but not the museum," Kamryn informed me.

"Have you guys been to a Major League Baseball game yet?" I asked the kids.

Little Kevin answered first. "Nope."

"No, Mommy hasn't taken us to any baseball games!" Kamryn exclaimed.

"I didn't know that you guys liked baseball," Ava was quick to say.

"But we've never said that we didn't like it, either," Little Kevin added.

"Okay, enough," Ava said abruptly, and then she turned her attention back toward me. "So, how long do you plan to be here?"

"Until Monday."

"Oh, Dad, why can't you stay longer?" Little Kevin chimed back in.

"Yeah, Daddy," Kamryn agreed.

"Because I've got things I need to take care of back home," I told them.

"You mean Ty and the baby?" Ava blurted out.

Puzzled, the kids looked at their mother and then back at me. "Who's Ty and the baby?" Little Kevin asked first.

"Yeah, who is that, Daddy?" Kamryn wanted to know.

"I'll talk to you guys about that later," I said, brushing Ava's comment off. Now wasn't the time to tell my kids about Ty and the baby. I was disappointed that Ava would bring that up at a time when I hadn't seen my kids in over four months. This time was for me and them to bond and catch up, not to talk about my other family. I certainly didn't want them thinking that I left them for Ty and the baby. That could really damage their self-esteem, and with what's going on with Little Kevin, I didn't want that added stress on him.

Ava exhaled a windstorm of breath and rolled her eyes. "So, where are you staying?" She decided to change the subject.

"I booked a hotel room downtown."

"Which one?"

"The Lancaster."

"Have you checked in yet?"

"No, I can't check in until after three, which is why I came here straight from the airport."

"So, what are you going to do in the meantime?"

"I was hoping I could chill here until then."

"Of course, you can, Dad. Let's go inside," Little Kevin insisted as he led the way.

"Yeah, Daddy, come on," Kamryn said as she grabbed my hand to lead me through the front doorway.

Paulina moved to the side, while Ava stood there and acted like she wasn't about to budge. But Kamryn moved right on by her mother, casually passing by her. Ava finally moved out of the way because she didn't want me brushing up against her.

"Take your shoes off," she grumbled as she rolled her eyes.

As requested, I took my shoes off by the front door. "Take your dad to the media room," Ava instructed the kids.

"Okay," Little Kevin replied.

As Little Kevin led me away from the door, he took me by a sweeping staircase leading to the second floor. The stairs, made of rich mahogany wood, had an intricately designed banister that added a touch of elegance. On the walls hung a series of expensive paintings, each one more captivating than the last. I swear, I never knew that Ava had such impeccable taste in art. The paintings, ranging from serene landscapes to abstract pieces, brought a vibrant yet tasteful burst of color to the space. The entryway itself was adorned with a large chandelier. It was a masterpiece in itself, with cascading crystals that sparkled and cast a warm, inviting glow throughout the space.

As we moved into the foyer, I noticed a beautifully carved console table, topped with an arrangement of fresh flowers in a crystal vase, adding a touch of elegance and freshness to the room. Beneath the table were top-of-the-line hardwood floors, which gleamed under the soft, ambient lighting. The dark walnut finish was polished to perfection, and it extended seamlessly throughout the house. The floor was complemented by the crown molding, which framed the ceilings; each detail was meticulously crafted and was painted a pristine white. The molding added a layer of refinement, enhancing the architectural beauty of the home.

As I was led out of the foyer, I entered the living room. It featured a luxurious velvet sofa in a deep shade of navy, paired with matching armchairs, which looked inviting enough to sink into. The coffee table, a sleek piece of glass and metal, was adorned with a few well-chosen decorative items, including a vase of fresh flowers, which added a touch of natural beauty. The room was anchored by a large, intricately patterned area rug, which added warmth and texture. The walls were painted in a soft, neutral palette, allowing the artwork and furniture to take center stage. Built-in bookshelves lined one wall and were filled with a curated collection of books and decorative items.

I have to admit that I wasn't shocked to see a grand piano sitting in the corner of this room. While we were living together back in Virginia, Ava had always harped on how she wanted one. I just never got around to getting one for her.

Moving on to the next room was the kitchen. It was huge.

A catering-style kitchen, with state-of-the-art appliances, sleek granite countertops, and a large island that sat in the center of the kitchen, with high-backed stools, creating a perfect spot for casual meals and conversations. The cabinets were made of the same rich wood as the floors, and they provided ample storage space, with accented brushed-style metal handles. The backsplash was made of intricately patterned tiles, adding a touch of artistry to the functional space. Copper pots and pans hung from a rack above the island, their warm tones adding to the inviting atmosphere. This room looked like a page out of a magazine.

Finally we went into the media room, and it was something you'd see on *MTV Cribs*. The first thing that caught my attention was the enormous projector screen on the wall, it was larger than life. It dominated the room, casting a faint glow that added to the surreal atmosphere. The surround sound speakers were discreetly embedded in the walls and promised an immersive audio experience.

Opposite the screen was a sprawling leather sectional sofa, its deep brown leather looking incredibly inviting. It was the kind of furniture you'd sink into and never want to leave. The sofa seemed to stretch endlessly, able to accommodate a large group comfortably, each seat perfectly positioned for an optimal view of the screen.

In the far-right corner of the room stood a minibar, its sleek design complemented the feel of the space. Bottles of top-shelf liquor lined the glass shelves, and a small refrigerator below held an assortment of beverages. There was even a gourmet popcorn maker with popcorn-designed paper bags sticking out the side holster of the machine. The media room gleamed under the recessed lighting, which was installed in the ceiling, casting a comfortable glow throughout the room. The attention to detail was astounding. This was a room designed for ultimate relaxation and entertainment, something you'd expect to see in a mansion owned by a Hollywood A-lister, not the home of my estranged wife.

I stood there taking it all in; a mixture of awe and jealousy bubbled inside of me. It was a lot to process, especially when I knew that she spent some of my ransom money to purchase this home.

"Sit down, Dad," Little Kevin instructed me.

I took a seat on the buttery smoothness of the leather sofa, and it made me feel like I was on cloud nine.

"Want me to make you some popcorn?" Kamryn volunteered as she sat on the sofa next to me. I looked back at the popcorn machine and immediately thought about the kernels getting stuck in my teeth. As I looked a few feet to the left of that machine, I eyed the minibar. The temptation to pour myself a drink popped in my mind, but I resisted, knowing that I was with my kids and now wasn't the time to do that.

"No, I'm fine, baby girl. Maybe next time," I told her.

"Whatcha want to watch on TV?" Little Kevin asked as he stood alongside me, with the television remote in his hand. I watched as he powered on the TV and sifted through the channels.

"I don't care really," I said. "Put on something you guys wanna watch," I suggested. "Speaking of which, isn't today a school day?" I added.

"Yes," Kamryn answered first.

"So, why aren't you guys in school?"

"Because Mommy picked us up early," Kamryn replied.

"Did you have doctor's appointments or something?"

"Nope. But a boy was bullying me on the bus this morning," Kamryn admitted.

"You two ride the same bus, right?" I asked.

"Yeah," Little Kevin finally chimed in.

"Well, where were you when the kid was bullying your sister?"

"I was in the back of the bus with my friends. But as soon as I heard him talking smack to her, I yelled at him and told him to leave her alone," Little Kevin explained.

I smiled like a proud dad. "That's my boy!" I commented, and slapped him on the arm.

Little Kevin finally settled on watching the latest *Planet of the Apes* movie. He and his sister crawled on the sofa and sat on the opposite sides of me. I placed my arms around the both of them and allowed them to rest in the crook of my arms. It felt so good to have my babies next to me. It felt like old times, and I was enjoying every second of this moment.

While we sat there, I occasionally peered around the media room and wondered how much money she forked out for everything. The more I thought about it, the more I became enraged. The fact that she pretended not to have any money was like a smack in the face. At the end of the day, all I want is my money, and before I leave, she will give it to me.

CHAPTER 13

Ava

PAULINA AND I HEADED OUT TO THE GARAGE SO WE COULD TALK IN private. "He thinks he's slick popping up at my house like this," I stated point-blank because I knew the real reason why Kevin had come. He could fool the kids and have them think he came here to see them, but I knew his real reason for coming. He wanted to see if he could twist my arm into giving him his part of the ransom money back. Like I said before, that would never happen. I suffered greatly for that money, and there was no way in hell that I would ever hand it back to him.

"Can you imagine how shocked I was to see him standing at the front door?" Paulina remarked.

"I was more shocked than you," I replied.

"Think he came here to see if you guys could reconcile?"

"Of course not," I replied, immediately shooting down that thought. I knew why he was really here, but I couldn't tell Paulina, because then I would have to explain to her what happened to Nick. That subject was off-limits. She could never know what happened that night.

"I think he still loves you."

"I couldn't care less about his love for me at this point. What

I'm concerned about is getting through this divorce and moving on with my life."

"Are you gonna let him stay for dinner?"

"No. As soon as three o'clock comes, I want him out of here. Until that time comes, I want you to be my eyes and ears. Make sure he doesn't try any funny business. He can only go to the bathroom and back out the front door. Understood?"

"Yes, ma'am."

"Okay, well, I'm gonna go in the media room and check on them," I told Paulina.

"Well, I'm gonna do the kids' laundry. So, if you need me, that's where I'll be."

"Roger that," I replied, and then we left the garage.

When I entered the media room, I zeroed in on Kevin and the kids. I could tell that he and the kids had missed each other. The scene with them sitting together, cradled in their father's arms, was picture-perfect. But in reality it wasn't. Kevin was a fucking scumbag, and our kids will soon find out how their dad broke up this family for a piece of ass. Now he has the audacity to show up and pretend like he's Father of the Year. I see right through his bullshit and I'm gonna tell him.

"I see you're making yourself at home," I commented as I stood in the middle of the floor.

"I'm just glad to be around my kids again," he answered, beaming.

"Yeah, I bet," I hissed. "Can I speak to you privately, if you don't mind?"

"Sure," he replied, and stood up from the sofa.

After he walked over to where I was standing, I escorted him into the kitchen, where we could have some privacy from the kids. "Have a seat," I insisted, pointing to the barstools placed around the island. "Want something to drink? Bottled water? Juice? Hot tea?"

"A bottle of water is fine," he noted after he sat down on one of the stools.

I grabbed a cold bottle of water from the fridge and handed it to him.

"Thank you," he said, and then he popped off the cap.

I stood on the opposite side of the island and looked Kevin dead-on and asked, "Why are you really here?"

He chortled. "I came here to see the kids."

"Bullshit, Kevin! You and I both know why you're here," I grumbled, shaking my head.

He flashed a fake smile. "Look, all I want is what's rightfully mine," he admitted.

"And I told you that I didn't have it." I didn't hesitate to lie.

"Come on, Ava, you think I'm stupid. Look at this freaking house you and the kids are living in. This place must have cost you at least a cool million, if not more. And if I recall, you didn't have a fucking dime when you left Virginia. At least that's what I thought until Little Kevin told me that Nick was the one who kidnapped him and Kammy. Now that the secret is out, I know for sure you got the ransom money. All I'm asking is for you to give me my part back. Nothing more, nothing less."

"Look, it's gone, okay? I spent it all," I finally admitted, hoping this would get him off my back and leave me alone about it.

"I don't believe you."

"Well, I did," I said with finality, hoping he'd just drop it and move on.

"I don't believe you spent all that money."

"Well, I did," I reiterated.

"What about the money you took from Nick?" he asked. That question hit me like a ton of bricks. How the hell did he know that I took money from Nick? Who was he talking to? And what did he know?

"I didn't take any money from Nick," I said with a straight face.

"Bullshit! The cops said that his safe was burglarized and his laptop was taken," Kevin growled. I could tell that he was getting frustrated with my lies.

"Are you broke or something?" I followed up, deliberately hurling an insult.

"Whether I'm broke or not is none of your concern. But I will tell you this, if I don't get my money before I leave town, there will be heavy consequences."

Hearing Kevin's words made my heart jerk in my chest, and I suddenly regretted bringing up this subject. I honestly wanted to ask him to leave, but I knew that it wouldn't sit well with the kids, so I held my tongue and began to ponder on how I was going to deal with him and this money situation. He had made it very apparent he wasn't going to leave it alone until I gave him something.

"So, whatcha gonna do, call the cops on me or something?" I wondered aloud.

"Try me," he said boldly.

I stood there, with my nostrils flaring, not knowing what to say or how to play this out, and then suddenly I felt the tension rise in my throat. I swear, it felt like he had my back up against the wall, and I didn't like that one bit. Usually, I always had the upper hand with Kevin. I was the dominant one in our marriage, even though he was the main breadwinner. But somehow, those roles have reversed, and I don't know how to handle it.

"So, what's it going to be?" he pressured.

I thought for a moment about how much cash I had on hand, because whether I wanted to or not, I realized I was going to have to give him something. "Look, I may have some cash laying around here, but I can't promise you it's the money you gave me for the ransom."

"Listen, Ava, I know you're sitting on a huge pile of cash, so stop playing games with me. All I'm asking for is my part of the ransom and I'm not leaving here until I get it," he announced. Then he stood up from the barstool and started walking away.

"Are you talking about today or when you leave town?" I asked him before he exited the kitchen.

"Before I leave town," he answered without looking back and disappearing around the corner.

CHAPTER 14

Ty

NORMALLY, WHEN KEVIN WENT OUT OF TOWN AND ARRIVED AT HIS destination, he'd call and check in. This time he hadn't done so, which was strange. He left at seven-thirty this morning, and now it's after one in the afternoon. I'm a little worried because this isn't like him. So, without giving it another thought, I dialed his cell phone number, and it rang five times before it went to voicemail. I hung up and immediately called him back. It rang five times before going to voicemail again. I called a third time, and it went straight to voicemail, and that gave me a cause for concern. Did Kevin just send me to voicemail deliberately? Or was he trying to call me at the same time I was trying to reach him? To find out the answer to that question, I called him back, and this time it rang four times before going to voicemail.

Instead of leaving him a message, I texted: **Kevin, where are you? Call me back. I'm beginning to worry.**

After I pressed the SEND button, I called my bestie, Whitney. She answered on the third ring. "What's up, girl?"

"Hey," I replied dryly.

"What's wrong?"

"Kevin left the house early this morning. He told me he was driving down to the Tidewater area to check on his store down there and look in on his house, and I haven't heard from him since. That's not like him."

"What time did he leave?"

"About seven-thirty."

"Damn, that's around six hours ago."

"I know."

"Have you tried calling him?"

"Of course, I have. I've called him, like, four times, and he didn't answer once, so I texted him. And now I'm just waiting for him to text me back."

"Did you guys resolve that issue from the other night?"

"Nope."

"Did you two argue before he left this morning?"

"I wouldn't call it an argument. But we did have some words," I acknowledged.

"Well, that's probably why he's not answering."

"You think so?"

"I know so. Men are petty like that. And when he gets back home later today, he's gonna act like he did nothing wrong."

"I swear, he better not go all day without calling me, or there's gonna be hell to pay when he gets back in here tonight."

"Do whatcha gotta do, girl! Because once you start letting a man disrespect you, that's how things are gonna be for the rest of your relationship."

"Not mine. Because I won't have it."

"Well, you better put your foot down now," Whitney advised me.

"Trust me, I will," I assured her.

"Good. That a girl," she cheered me on, which was what she did best. She and I made small talk about her man and then we started talking about when I was going back to work. I told her that I had taken an extended leave from the airlines because I wasn't ready to leave my baby yet. I also told her I was thinking about eventually quitting altogether, since Kevin just landed a lucrative new auto parts partnership.

"Never, ever depend on a man to fully take care of you. It's not gonna end well. Believe you me," she warned.

Despite what Whitney advised, I was a big girl, and I knew what was best for me and my daughter. Kevin was a great provider, and I knew that Annabelle and I would be well taken care of. If need be, I could start a side business and get Kevin to fund it. I wasn't no dumb chick at all. I knew how to get to the bag, so me and my baby would never be without.

Whitney and I talked for a few more minutes and then I told her I'd call her later. After we hung up, I tried calling Kevin's cell phone again, but for the fifth time, he didn't answer. This made my blood boil. I left another text message, but this time I made sure he would feel the venom in my words:

Kevin, you need to call me as soon as you read this message. Now I don't know what's going on in your mind that would make you think you don't have to check in. It's been six hours since you left, and I know for a fact that our little spat isn't causing you to do this. If you are avoiding me, then you're gonna have a problem when you get home. I'll be waiting. You better call me!

CHAPTER 15

Kevin

I GOT THE KIDS TO PACK SWIMWEAR AND ENOUGH CLOTHES FOR THREE days, since it was almost time for me to go to the hotel to check in. The kids were excited to hang out with me for the weekend, and I was excited, too. After they had their overnight bags in hand, Ava stood at the front door to see us off. She kissed both of the kids and told them to be good. They both assured her that they would behave.

"I wanna talk to you guys every night before you go to bed," Ava said, looking directly at them, avoiding eye contact with me.

"Don't worry, I will make sure they call you," I swore.

She gave me a half smile and said, "Okay."

I know for a fact that she gnashed a few teeth before mustering up the energy to respond. I laughed on the inside because I made her do something she didn't want to do. It was evident she was still upset from our earlier conversation about her returning my money to me. But the way I look at it, that was her problem because I'm not letting up. I want my money, and she'd better deliver.

Ava and Paulina waved goodbye from the entryway of the front door as I backed out of the driveway and drove away. Having the kids in my possession gave me a sense of control. I realized this was the beginning of a new chapter in my life. From this day going forward, my children would be with me all the time, and I would have the final say when it comes to making the decisions for them. The first thing I planned to do was get Little Kevin some well-needed help from a therapist. Ava wouldn't be around to stop me.

As soon as I arrived at the hotel, I checked in, and after the kids and I put our things inside the room, I suggested that we go to the pool. They were excited by the idea and swapped out of their regular clothes and into their swimsuits within minutes. After they grabbed towels from the bathroom, we headed out of the room. I led Little Kevin and Kamryn through the lobby of the hotel, holding Kamryn's hand as we made our way to the outdoor pool area.

The Texas sun was bright and warm, casting a golden glow over the sparkling blue water. As soon as we reached the pool, Little Kevin shot off, while Kamryn broke free from my grip, kicked off her shoes, and jumped into the pool with a huge splash.

I smiled as I watched them for a moment before I headed to a nearby lounge chair. I settled in, took a deep breath, and pulled out my cell phone. The screen lit up with multiple missed calls and a long text message from Ty. Anxiety struck me for a moment, knowing that I was going to have some explaining to do when I eventually got on the phone with her. I'd have to break it to her that I wasn't coming home until Monday.

Curious about the contents of her text message, I opened the text and read it in its entirety. From the looks of things, Ty didn't seem too happy right now, especially since I hadn't answered any of her calls. She thought it had something to do with that disagreement we had before I left home this morning. I guess, I'm gonna have a great deal of explaining to do.

I sighed heavily as my fingers hovered for a few seconds over her phone number. Then it dawned on me that I've got to get into a certain headspace to deal with her, and I wasn't in the right frame of mind for that right now, because for one, I was with my kids, and I had other business to handle first. So that's what I intended to do.

Switching to my contacts, I scrolled down and tapped on Lacey's name. The phone rang twice before she picked up.

"Hey, Kevin," Lacey answered, her voice was smooth and calm, showing no hint of the dangerous plans she and Maceo had on the horizon.

"Just called to let you know that I made it to Houston, and I've got the kids with me," I said, glancing over at Little Kevin and Kamryn, who were laughing and playing in the water. "They're out of the house, so you and your guy can go in freely."

"Sounds good," Lacey replied, a hint of satisfaction in her tone. "Any security I should know about?"

"Yeah, she has security cameras around the entire house. Plus, a Ring cam," I noted, lowering my voice. "And to get to her place, you have to drive down a long driveway. Her house sits on three acres of land."

There was a brief pause on the other end. "All right, thanks for the heads-up."

I nodded, though she couldn't see me. "Just make sure it's quick and clean. I don't want anything traced back to me."

"Don't worry. We've got this under control," Lacey assured me.

"All right. Well, if you need anything else, just call me."

"Sure thing," she replied, and then we ended the call.

Immediately after I pressed the END button, I glanced over at the pool, where my kids were having the time of their lives, completely unaware of the dark undertones of the conversation I just had with the person who put a bounty on their mother's head. For a second I felt guilty, but then I quickly pushed it aside because I had to stay focused.

After pocketing my cell phone, I laid back in the lounge chair, pretending to be just another dad enjoying a sunny day by the pool with my kids. But my mind was far from relaxed because I was already calculating the next steps in my perilous game. Getting my money from Ava was my main focus.

After swimming for more than two hours, the kids mentioned they were hungry, so they climbed out of the pool and went back to the room to shower and change into some dry clothes. Once they showered, they got dressed, one by one, in the bathroom, and when they were done, I told them to give me a second while I used the potty.

"Ewww . . . Daddy, you're too big to be saying you gotta use the *potty,*" Kamryn joked.

Little Kevin chuckled. "Yeah, Dad, that's for babies. Even we don't say that anymore."

"Ah, you guys give your old man a break, will ya?" I said, waving them off and heading into the bathroom.

It didn't take me long to do what I had to do, so I was in and out in less than a minute. As soon as I opened the bathroom door, I heard my daughter say, "Hold on, let me get him. He's in the bathroom."

With a puzzled look on my face, I walked toward my daughter and whispered, "Who is that?"

"Some lady named Ty," she replied innocently.

Dread and trepidation instantly consumed me, and my heart sank as my daughter held out my cell phone for me to take. I knew I couldn't put this off any longer—Ty was now aware that I was in Houston with the kids. She wasn't going to be happy about it, either, especially since she was just now finding out. I braced myself for the wrath I was about to feel.

"Hello," I said hesitantly.

"Don't *hello* me, Kevin. And please don't tell me that you're in Houston right now," she boomed, her voice stern and full of rage.

"Why don't you just calm down before the baby hears you," I advised her, hoping she'd take heed and think about our child.

"No, fuck that! You're always telling me, 'Watch your tone around the baby,' using that line to keep me from fussing your ass out. Now tell me why you lied to me and said you were going to Tidewater, when you knew you were going to Houston, Texas, the entire time? What's going on with you? Why are you keeping me in the dark about everything that's going on with you?" Ty's voice was sharp and accusatory.

I was sure the kids could hear Ty's voice through the phone. She was extremely loud, so I paused for a second and glanced around at them to see if I was correct. What do you know, Kamryn was watching me, but Little Kevin sat on a small couch, watching TV. So I looked back at Kamryn, smiled, and gave her a little wink, reassuring her that everything was all right. "Look, I wanted to tell you, but I knew it was going to be a problem, so I figured I'd tell you after I got here," I finally answered, my tone low and neutral.

"So that's your excuse?"

"It's not an excuse, Ty. It's actually the truth."

"Screw the truth, Kevin. I don't wanna hear about you telling me the truth. Because for the last few days, I haven't been getting the truth from you. As a matter of fact, I haven't been getting anything from you. You've been mum about everything that's going on in your life, and I don't like it!" she screeched, her voice forceful and to the point.

"Can we talk about this later?" I asked nicely.

"No! We are going to talk *now*. I need to know all about these secrets you've been keeping from me. And before you hang up this phone, you're gonna tell me why the hell you snuck out to Texas without telling me," she roared, and I could feel the tension building.

I clenched my jaw, trying to maintain my composure, especially around my kids. The last thing I wanted was for them to see me upset. "Ty, I'm not keeping any secrets from you. Okay! Things have been really hectic with me lately and I just need some time to sort them out."

"Bullshit, Kevin! You're hiding something from me and I'm gonna find out what it is!" she stated, her frustration was clear.

I took a deep breath, trying to keep my voice steady. "Ty, there's nothing to find out. My kids are here in the hotel room with me, and they are watching me. So I will call you back later after they go to bed," I said with finality.

"No, you owe me an explanation right now!" she snapped, and a few minutes later, I heard faint cries in the background of Annabelle crying.

"See, you woke the baby up," I pointed out, trying to speak as low as I could.

"Don't worry about her. She's fine. *I'm the one* you need to worry about," she barked as Annabelle's cries got louder.

I immediately felt my composure fraying, but I knew I couldn't lose my cool in front of the kids. "Ty, I'm gonna need you to lower your voice and go and attend to Annabelle right now. I'll call you back later."

"Don't you dare hang up on me, Kevin!" Her voice was shrill now, and I noticed Little Kevin casting a concerned glance in my direction.

I closed my eyes briefly, taking another deep breath, and then I said, "Ty, I have to go. I'll call you back." Without waiting for her response, I ended the call, feeling a mix of frustration and relief.

I pocketed my cell phone, looked over at my kids, and forced another smile. "You guys ready to go eat?"

Kamryn jumped up from the bed and shouted, "Yeah, Daddy! Let's go!"

Little Kevin casually stood up from the sofa. "Where are we going?"

"Where would you guys like to go?" I asked them both.

"Let's get pizza!" Kamryn blurted out with excitement.

"I'd rather eat a cheeseburger with some onion rings and a chocolate milk shake," Little Kevin chimed in.

"Well, I'll tell you what, we're gonna find a place where they sell them both. Okay?"

"Yay!" Kamryn shouted with joy.

Little Kevin nodded his head in a cool manner.

On our way out of the hotel room, Kamryn walked alongside, while Little Kevin walked ahead of us. As we made our way to the elevator, Kamryn asked, "Who is Ty?"

"She's a friend," I answered without giving it much thought. I didn't mean to lie to her, it just came out that way.

"Well, who is Annabelle?" Her questions continued.

Caught off guard, I thought for a moment about how to answer it. I knew I couldn't lie to her about who Annabelle was, because Kamryn would come back later and remind me about the lie. So I exhaled and said, "It's a long story and I will tell you about her soon enough."

"Okay," Kamryn replied, responding as if my answer had been sufficient enough.

We strolled inside the elevator, took it down to the first floor, walked through the lobby, hand in hand, as Little Kevin continued to lead the way. Outside we waited for the valet to bring the car. As soon as he arrived, I slipped him a tip while the kids and I climbed inside, and then I pulled off into the sunset. It was nothing but up from here. I could feel it in my bones.

CHAPTER 16

Ty

INFURIATED BY THE WAY KEVIN DISMISSED ME, I SLAMMED MY CELL phone down on the nightstand in our bedroom and stormed into Annabelle's room to tend to her. I knew it was feeding time, so I grabbed her from her crib, carried her over to my rocking chair in the opposite corner of the room, sat there, and then I started feeding her. She calmed down immediately after I stuck my nipple in her mouth.

Unfortunately for me, I couldn't calm my emotions down, especially after the way Kevin treated me. I mean, how dare he leave and fly out to Texas without telling me? What the hell was wrong with him? Was I not important enough in his life to know his whereabouts? I know one thing for sure. Something wasn't right with this whole situation and he was keeping a secret from me. The fact that I heard him talking about Ava and the nanny to someone, and now he was out there, just didn't sit right with me.

My intuition is telling me that something is about to go down, and since he doesn't want to tell me what it is, maybe I should be calling Ava and telling her what I know . . .

I finally willed myself to calm down while feeding Annabelle. Thankfully, she went right back to sleep, so I placed her back inside the crib and crept out of her room quietly to prevent from waking her back up.

Upon entering my bedroom, I crawled on the bed, grabbed my cell phone, and sifted through my contact list, where I had saved Ava's number from that one time she called me after finding out about my and Kevin's affair. I took a deep breath, exhaled, and then I dialed her number.

Surprisingly, she answered on the first ring. "Yes," she said. It was as if she, too, had saved my number in her contacts and for some reason had been waiting for my call.

"Hello, um, this is Ty, Kevin's—" My words were immediately cut off by Ava.

"I know who you are. How can I help you?" she hissed.

"Look, Ava, I'm sure this is awkward for you, and I am the last person you wanna talk to right now, but I'm calling you because I think there's something you should know."

There was a brief pause at the other end of the line before Ava responded, her tone cautious. "I'm listening."

"A few nights ago, I overheard Kevin talking to someone on a phone call," I began to say, choosing my words carefully. "He was talking about you, and it didn't sound good."

"What did he say?"

"Well, I came in on the tail end of the conversation, so the part I heard was when he asked the person on the other end whether they were going to take you away from the house or were they going to do it there. Whatever it means. Then he told them that a nanny lived with you, but she would be easy to get rid of. So, immediately after he got off the phone, I asked him who had he been talking to, and he refused to tell me. The only answer he gave me was that the less I know, the better off I'll be. That didn't sit well with me. I'd never seen him be so secretive about anything until lately. And to put the nail in the coffin, did you know that I didn't know he was flying out there to see the kids?"

"No, I didn't know that," Ava replied, her voice low.

"Well, I just found out today when I called and your baby girl answered the phone. I swear, I was livid. He left the house this morning pretending to go to the Tidewater area to check on his store and the house you guys own."

"That's not good," Ava continued. Her tone sounded nonchalant. It almost seemed like she was trying to figure out if I was credible or not.

"Listen, Ava, I know this is a lot to take in, and I'm sure you may not believe me, but I wouldn't be bringing this to your attention if this wasn't weighing heavily on me. In my mind I just wanted to be safe, not sorry," I explained.

Ava cleared her throat and then said, "Ty, if you want me to be honest with you, I am most certainly taken aback by this information and I'm trying to sort it out in my mind. I'm also trying to figure out what are you looking to gain by telling me this?"

"I'm not looking to gain anything. Like I said a few minutes ago, after hearing that conversation, it had been on my mind, and every time I tried to get Kevin to tell me what was going on, he would shut me down, and I didn't like it. The fact that he left Virginia to fly out there without telling me is a telltale sign that he's up to something. Now, if you choose to disregard what I'm saying, Ava, that's on you. I did my part. My conscience is clear."

"Okay, fair enough. And just so you know, I appreciate you bringing this to my attention." Ava thanked me.

"No problem. I'm sure you would've done it for me as well," I replied.

"I'm sure I would've."

"Oh, and so you know, Kevin told me about the incident with Little Kevin and his best friend, Nick."

"That doesn't surprise me."

"Well, I just want you to know that secret is safe with me," I declared.

"I sure would appreciate that," Ava responded flatly.

"Can I say one more thing before I go?"

"Sure."

"Can you keep this between us?"

"I was going to do that anyway," Ava pointed out.

"I appreciate that," I stated.

"Take care."

"You do the same."

After I ended the call, I laid my head back on the pillow. Knowing that I did what needed to be done, I felt a sense of relief and that a weight was lifted off my shoulders. The situation was out of my hands now. It was up to Ava to take the reins on this matter.

CHAPTER 17

Ava

Alarmed by the call I received from Kevin's girlfriend, Ty, I sat in my chair in my home office, replaying every word she had uttered from her mouth. Nothing she said seemed far-fetched, especially considering Kevin's recent behavior. I believed everything she said, but given the fact that Kevin was now sharing the same bed with her, why would she betray him for me? That part seemed odd. In my mind there was either trouble in paradise or the girl had a conscience. Either way I wasn't taking the information she'd given me lightly. One way or another, I was going to get to the bottom of things, because at this point it seemed like my life depended on it.

In deep thought I couldn't help but wonder who Kevin could've been talking to on the phone when Ty started to eavesdrop on his conversation. Then it hit me that it couldn't have been anyone else but Nick's sister, Lacey. She and Kevin have always been tight over the years. I remember Kevin telling me that she used to have a crush on him when they were growing up. But since he and Nick were like brothers, she was always off-limits to him, which was another reason why she hated my guts so much after I left Nick to be with Kevin. Knowing all of this, I wouldn't be surprised if Kevin and Lacey are plotting something against me.

Ty said that she overheard Kevin ask the caller if they were taking me out of the house or doing "it" here. The only thing I can think "it" means is *killing me.* Then going on to say that I had a nanny, but she would be easy to get rid of, was the final piece of the puzzle—not to mention the fact that he showed up here without giving me a moment's notice. What I can't figure out is . . . why would Kevin have me killed? What had he told Lacey? Does she know that I have Nick's laptop and his money? Does she want it back? I also wanna know when is this supposed to go down? This weekend while the kids are gone with Kevin?

Yeah, he thinks he's so fucking slick, coming out here like he missed the kids and wanted to spend time with them. All the while, setting me up. Fucking loser! Well, I have a trick up my sleeve for him. I will not go down without a fight. And when it's all said and done, I might be the last one standing.

I was brimming inside with anxiety as I thought about the unknown. The reason I left Virginia in the first place was so that I didn't have to look over my shoulder all the time and I could start a new, peaceful life. The thought of living in constant fear and with paranoia wasn't how I wanted to spend the rest of my life. Now that I'm armed with this new information, I'm forced to go back into survival mode. Unfortunately for me, I've got to fight alone. It's now me, myself, and I against whoever tries to come through my front door.

"Mrs. Frost, are you in here?" Paulina called from the other side of the door as she knocked on it gently.

"Yes, come on in," I instructed her.

As she pushed the door of my home office open, I looked directly into her innocent face and wondered what would happen to her if I allowed someone to come inside the house and hurt her. This woman was like a mother to me and has been with me since the kids were small. She was now family to me, so it would tear my heart apart if something happened to her on my watch. I have to protect her at all costs. And that's exactly what I intend to do.

"I was wondering if you wanted me to make you something to eat, since the kids aren't here?" she started off saying while standing in the entryway of my office.

"Isn't there still some leftover enchiladas in the fridge?" I asked.

"Yes, there's a few left," she replied.

"Well, then that's what I'll eat."

"Okay, so I'll take them out and warm them up in the oven for you," she volunteered.

"Thank you, Paulina!"

"No problem, ma'am," Paulina answered, and as she was about to turn around to leave, I stopped her in her tracks.

"You miss the kids, don't you?" I asked.

She beamed from ear to ear. "Is it that noticeable?"

I cracked a smile. "Yes, it is."

"It's kind of weird that they're not here right now." Paulina looked down at her wristwatch. "Right about now, they would be running around here, playing hide and seek."

"I know," I agreed as I thought about them running around and hiding from each other. I loved seeing them play together. I've noticed that since their kidnapping, they have grown closer.

"Well, don't worry, they will be back soon enough," Paulina said.

"Yeah, they will," I concurred. "Hey, let me ask you something."

"Yes, ma'am."

"Would you like to go see your family for a few days?" This plan just popped up in my head. I figured that if I got her out of the house, I could be alone to figure this thing out on my own.

"To Mexico?" she wondered aloud.

"Yes."

"Most of my family are in Texas now, ma'am."

"Well, would you like to go and visit them?" I pressed the issue.

"Um, well, I could, but I need to call them first to make sure it's okay."

"That's fine. Let me know, because I'm cool with giving you a few days off. You deserve it," I insisted. I figured trying to get her out of the house this way wouldn't raise any suspicions on her part. I don't need Paulina obsessing about anything I've got going on, because she doesn't know how to deal with volatile situations like I do. So, why subject her to it? The quicker I can get her out of this house, the better I can deal with the possible target on my back and be done with it.

After Paulina left to go warm up the enchiladas, I sat there and tried to figure out what my next move should be. I needed a gun to protect myself, so I called the arms dealer I just met to see if he could help me. I dialed his number. He finally answered on the fourth ring.

"Hello," he said.

"Hi, Neil, this is Ava. How are you?"

"I'm good. What a pleasant surprise," he stated. He seemed happy to hear from me.

"I know it's been a minute. I've been busy with the kids and trying to manage some things I have on my plate."

"Understandable."

"Well, the reason for my call is I need a favor from you."

"Sure, what is it?"

"I don't want to say over the phone. Mind if we meet in person?"

"Sure, when?"

"As soon as you're available."

"Well, I'm on my way home now from running errands, but I can redirect my GPS if you give me your location."

"I'll tell you what, meet me in the parking lot of the Panera Bread on Jefferson Davis in fifteen minutes."

"I'm about twenty minutes away from there as we speak."

"Okay, well, I'll see you in twenty."

"Roger that," he replied, and then we disconnected the call.

Heading out of the house, I told Paulina to stop cooking the enchiladas, I had an important errand to take care of.

Neil and I met at Panera Bread, like we discussed. I arrived a few minutes before he got there. Dressed in golf attire from head to toe, he climbed out of his late-model white-and-gold Porsche Panamera. I smiled as I climbed out of my car to greet him.

"Good to see you," he said as he embraced me with a hug.

"Good to see you, too," I told him.

"So, what's up?" he asked, getting straight to the point.

"Come on, let's take a walk," I suggested.

"Okay," he replied.

As we started walking around the parking lot of the shopping center, I began to muster up the gumption to ask him about helping me get a firearm. I wasn't sure how he'd take it, but I knew I had to have this conversation with him. I cleared my throat as I thought of every possible way to break the ice with this conversation.

"Is everything okay?" He seemed concerned with my hesitation.

"Yes . . . I mean, no. Not really," I started off saying as we walked side by side around the parking lot.

"What's going on?"

Feeling the weight of my situation bearing down on my shoulders, I glanced around, making sure no one was within earshot. When I realized I was good to speak, I lowered my voice and leaned in closer. "I need some protection," I finally said.

"What kind of protection?" He seemed confused.

"Whatever you can get me," I said boldly, hoping he would catch my drift.

"You mean a firearm?" He wanted to be clear.

"Yes," I replied.

"Are you in any danger right now?" He was probing me for more answers.

Stunned by his question, I chuckled nervously and said, "No. Of course not." I mean, I couldn't tell him that my husband was setting me up to be killed, because I didn't know it for certain. I also didn't want to scare him off by telling him about the conversation I had with Ty. So I figured if I told him that I only needed the gun to protect my house, since I was out here alone, maybe he'd be more likely to help me.

"Look, I'm out here in this city alone, so I just need something I can handle that will protect my house while my kids and I are asleep at night."

"Why don't you go to one of the local gun shops? Most of them have shooting ranges located inside and you could test out the firearms you like," he suggested.

"I can't. I'm a convicted felon," I confessed.

Shocked at my admission, Neil's eyes grew in size and his mouth widened as he said, "Wow! I would not have ever guessed. What did you do?"

Mixed with both anxiety and wanting to be cautious of what I say to him, I quickly came up with a plausible story about my past, but without telling him how deep I was in the world of car theft. "About fifteen years ago, I was driving a car I thought belonged to a guy I was dating at the time. Come to find out, the car was stolen. So he and I were both hauled off to jail. I served a couple of years in the can because I refused to rat him out and, of course, got more time because he was a two-time felon," I explained, but only giving him the half-truth.

"So you liked bad boys, huh?" he joked.

"I did at one point," I confessed.

"Have you thought about getting your rights back so that you can purchase a gun?"

Frustrated by his way of trying to find me other resources, I sucked my teeth and said, "Look, I've looked into all of that. But that's gonna take some time and I need a gun now."

"Well, I don't know if I can help you."

Disappointed by Neil's lack of support, I blinked rapidly, my heart thundering in my chest, as I began to lose patience with this guy. Did he not see the desperation in my eyes? Did I not tell him that I needed this firearm to protect my family? Was he not taking me seriously? I bet you if I offered to fuck him, he'd be willing and able to help me. I swear, men are freaking pieces of shit. But I couldn't blow my cool. I knew if I leaned on him harder, he'd come around. So a strong desire propelled me forward and I convinced myself that I had to be aggressive now or never.

I swallowed the lump that had formed at the back of my throat and got up the courage to say, "Listen, Neil, I need this badly. Trust me, if I could go to someone else, I would."

I could see the reluctance on Neil's face as I arched my eyebrows at him. He acted like he wanted to run off in the opposite direction, and never look back. But then his facial expression changed. I was beginning to see hope in his eyes.

He eventually leaned in my direction, his expression earnest. "Can I trust you?"

"Absolutely," I said with confidence.

He studied me for a moment and then nodded. "Okay, I'll

help you, but I need to know you're not going to use what I give you for the wrong reasons. My reputation and my life depend on discretion."

"Neil, I promise, you will not regret this," I reassured him.

"I'm gonna hold you to that," he replied. Then he went into a spiel about how important it was for me not to tell anyone that he was helping me get a gun. I promised him that I wouldn't. He then started asking me questions about if I knew how to load, unload, and shoot a gun. I assured him that I did. I even told him that I preferred a 9mm Glock or a Ruger LC9.

"What do you know about those guns?"

"I told you I used to date bad boys, so I know how to use those guns."

"Well, I could get you either of the two. But it's gonna cost you about five hundred dollars. Ammo will be separate."

"When do you need the money?" I wanted to know.

"As soon as you can get it to me."

"Okay. I can go to the ATM and pull it out now," I mentioned as I peered around the parking lot to see if I could see a Bank of America ATM within eyesight. I didn't see one, but there was a Wells Fargo cash machine on the other side of the parking lot. "There's an ATM over there." I pointed in the direction in which I wanted Neil to look. "I can go right there and pull the money out."

"That'll be fine," he replied.

After getting the green light from Neil, we walked back to our cars and drove separately to the ATM. He sat in his car and watched as I withdrew the money I was going to give him. I took exactly seven hundred dollars out and when I had it in hand, I gave it to Neil with high hopes that he would return later with my gun and ammo. "I know I only met you a few days ago, but I trust that you won't take my money and run off with it," I said.

He chuckled as he sat in the driver's seat of his car. "You'll never have to worry about that from me. And to prove it, I'm gonna let you take a screenshot of my car registration and my driver's license," he insisted.

I pulled out my cell phone and took screenshots of his registration and driver's license. Immediately after, he agreed to meet me in a day or so. "But I'm gonna call you first," he stated.

"Okay, then, I'll wait for your call," I replied.

"Sounds good," he added, and then we parted ways.

CHAPTER 18

Kevin

After a busy and adventurous day, the kids and I went back to my hotel room and settled down for the rest of the night. I allowed them to watch television after they changed into their pj's. While they were immersed in the movie that was playing, Ava called to say good night to them. The conversation between them only lasted a couple of minutes, and when I thought Little Kevin was about to hang up the call, he passed the phone to me and told me that his mother wanted to speak with me. I took the phone and casually said hello.

"How did they act today?" she asked.

"They were pretty good."

"What did you feed them?"

"We got some pizza, a couple of cheeseburgers, fries and onion rings, and they had ice cream afterward."

"You didn't buy them any candy, did you?"

"Of course not. Kamryn tried to get me to get her some. But I didn't give in."

"Good job."

"I appreciate you saying that," I acknowledged.

"You're welcome," Ava said. Then she changed the subject. "So let me ask you a question."

"Go ahead."

"Are you expecting me to give you the ransom money in cash?"

"Of course not. How would that work with me catching a plane ride back to Virginia. I wanted you to make the transfer to my bank account."

"Oh, okay."

"So, do you got it?"

"I'm working on it."

"Well, you got until I leave on Monday."

"Is that when you're bringing the kids back?"

"Yes."

"Think I could hang out with you guys while you're here?"

Caught off guard by her question, I paused for a moment. I mean the original plan was to get my kids and keep them out of sight while Lacey and her crew planned their attack on Ava. But if I allow her to hang out with us, that could possibly derail any plans Lacey and her hit man have come up with, and I'm not trying to do that. I can't risk the safety of my children or myself because Ava wants to have a family reunion. She gave up that luxury when she said she didn't want us to be a family anymore and filed for divorce.

"So, can I meet up with you guys or what?" she asked again. "Whenever it's convenient with you."

"Um, I'll let you know," I told her.

"You know you don't have to be at the hotel if you don't want to be. You can stay here at my house if you like," she offered.

"Oh no, I'm good. But I appreciate the gesture," I said.

"You sure? Because I have a nice guest room you could sleep in." She wouldn't let up.

"No, I'm good. But I appreciate you even welcoming me into your home."

"Well, if you change your mind, the offer is still on the table."

"I'll keep that in mind."

"Okay, I'm gonna go. But have the kids call me in the morning when they get up."

"Will do," I assured her, and then I pressed the END button.

After I hung up with Ava, I sat there baffled at how, out of the blue, she wanted to be nice and offer for me to stay at her home. Just a few days ago, she wouldn't return my call. Now I can stay in her home while I'm in Houston. Something is telling me that she's got something up her sleeve. I'm curious to know what it is.

Not too long after the kids fell asleep, I reluctantly picked up the phone and called Ty. She had called me about five times within the last hour, so I knew she wasn't going to rest until she got me on the phone tonight. I dialed her cell phone number and headed toward the balcony of the hotel room. Instantly my legs felt like two lead pipes as I swayed from side to side, signaling to me that dread was to come. Each step seemed labored, as if walking into chaos. As soon as I walked onto the balcony, she answered and I stopped walking. I swear, my underarms became drenched with sweat and my stomach started developing knots inside.

"Hello," she said with an attitude.

Already dreading the conversation, I put on my thinking cap because I knew I had to continue covering my tracks from the lies I had told her previously.

"Hey, baby, I'm returning your call."

Ty's silence on the other end of the line was deafening. After a moment she replied, "After I had to call you at least five times."

"The kids and I were out. We just got back to the hotel room and now they are asleep."

Ty took a deep breath and then she exhaled. "Kevin, why didn't you tell me you were going to Houston? And tell me the truth this time."

I hesitated, trying to construct my lie carefully, but then I figured, why bother? It wasn't going to work. Everything I've been telling her up until now hasn't been the truth—and she knows it, and hasn't been happy about it, either.

"Ty, do we have to go through this again?" I finally said. I refused to revisit that conversation we had earlier.

"What's with all the secrecy? And the lies?"

"I haven't lied to you."

"You haven't been telling me the truth," she insisted.

"Look, can we talk about something else? Because I'm beginning to feel drained from this whole thing."

"So you're gonna avoid this conversation at all costs, huh?"

"I just don't want to get into it right now."

"And I'm never gonna know who you were talking to on the phone the other night, either, huh?"

"I told you, the less you know, the better off you'll be."

"Enough, Kevin! If you won't be honest with me, then there's nothing more to say." Ty's voice was cold and final.

"Let's not end our conversation like this."

"Too late for all that. And I'm gonna say this before I hang up: Don't call me if you get into some shit you can't get out of," she roared, and then abruptly hung up the phone, leaving me staring at mine. Any other time I would've called her back, but not tonight. I had more important things on my mind and arguing with her wasn't one of them. I eventually tossed the phone onto the bed and thought nothing else about the conversation.

CHAPTER 19

Ava

WHAT TY TOLD ME HAD TO BE TRUE. THERE WAS NO WAY THAT Kevin would have ever not wanted to take the opportunity for him and me to spend time with the kids together as a family. Something was definitely going down and I was going to find out.

It was a quiet Saturday and I was working in my home office. I occasionally looked at the security cameras throughout the entire house, noticing Paulina on one of the screens humming softly to herself as she cleaned the windows in Little Kevin's bedroom. I've noticed throughout the years how she has always cleaned my house so effortlessly. She's always been so good at her job. So, as I watched her wipe the glass clean with smooth, methodical strokes, I realized that something had immediately caught her attention. Then a few seconds later, she took her eyes off whatever it was and continued cleaning.

Being the nosey person I am, I perused through the camera's angles on my monitor on the left wing of the house to see what had caught Paulina's attention. That's when I noticed a black car, with heavily tinted windows, parked across the street alongside my neighbors' lawn. I didn't put too much thought into the car being there, until about thirty minutes later, after realizing I hadn't seen any movement the entire time I had been sitting there.

To make sure that I wasn't being paranoid, I played back the video from that camera angle to when the car first pulled up and saw that no one had ever exited it. This alarmed me big-time. So I hit the control key for that particular camera and zoomed in on the car, hoping I could get a better look. The only thing I got was movement. I could tell that someone was still inside the car, but I couldn't get a clear visual of the person. I honestly couldn't tell if it was a man or a woman, and this didn't sit right with me.

Disturbed by this, I switched camera screens on the monitor to locate Paulina and saw that she had just placed the cleaning supplies in the closet downstairs and was making her way to the kitchen. I got up from my chair and followed her there. When I entered the kitchen, she was preparing a sandwich for herself. The smell of grilled cheese sandwiches filled the air.

"Hey, Paulina," I called out, trying to keep my voice calm. "There's a car outside and it's been sitting there for a while now, and no one has gotten out of it."

Paulina took the grilled cheese sandwich out of the pan with a spatula and placed the sandwich on a nearby plate. "What kind of car?" she asked, wiping her hands on a towel and walking over to where I was standing.

"It's a black car, with tinted windows, and it's parked outside of Little Kevin's bedroom window," I replied, my eyes widened with concern.

"Oh yeah, I saw it when it first pulled up," she acknowledged. Then she followed me to the living-room area of the house to peer out the window.

"Don't you find it odd that no one has gotten out of it?" I asked her.

"I didn't notice."

"Well, it's making me feel like whoever's in that car may be watching my home."

"So, what are you going to do?" Paulina asked.

"I'm gonna go out there and pretend like I'm going to the mailbox, to see how they react," I told her, and then I proceeded toward the front door.

With great strides, I exited my home and pretended to be looking at something on my cell phone as I walked down the driveway toward the mailbox. The plan was to act as if I was going to check to see if I had mail and not once look in the direction of the car until after I looked inside the mailbox. I knew I would have to count on my peripheral vision to see any sudden movement coming from the car.

When I arrived at the mailbox, I opened the latch and peeped inside. After a few seconds I closed it. Immediately after, I turned around and casually glanced at everything in my line of vision, and then I did a double take, as if this was my first time seeing the car. I did this to see if the person in the car would make a sudden move, but whoever was inside didn't even flinch. So I squinted my eyes as if I was readjusting them to get a better look, hoping once again this would force the driver to make a move, but again it didn't. This got me to thinking that the driver was either asleep or bold. I knew realistically that the person behind the wheel wasn't asleep because he or she had just gotten there.

On the fly, I made a daring decision to walk toward the car. I figured that the person in the car was going to do one of two things. Either he or she was going to roll down the window and show me themselves or leave before I could get a chance to see who it was.

As I headed in the direction of the car, my heart jackhammered against my sternum with each step I took. When I had gotten halfway to the middle of the street, the car's engine roared to life, breaking the silence with a startling ferocity. I froze for a moment as the car sped off down the street, kicking up dust and gravel in its wake. I stood there with my cell phone in hand and snapped a couple of photos of the license plate. After I watched the car disappear down the road, my mind started racing with questions and fears.

When I turned around and headed back inside the house, Paulina was waiting anxiously at the front door for me. She could tell that I wasn't okay with what had just happened.

"I saw them when they sped off. Did you get a chance to see the driver?" she asked, her voice trembling.

"No, I couldn't see anything. The tint was too dark," I replied, my tone grim and frustrated.

"Who do you think that could've been?" Paulina's face went pale.

"I don't know."

"Should we call the police?"

I hesitated, considering my options. "No, not yet," I finally said. "Let's just keep an eye on things for now. I'll keep checking the security cameras periodically and stay on the lookout, just in case they want to show back up. In the meantime let's keep the doors locked and stay vigilant."

Paulina nodded, her expression serious. "I'll keep my eyes opened at all times, don't you worry," she promised, returning to the kitchen, where she had left her grilled cheese sandwich.

I headed back to my home office and replayed the camera footage for the next twenty minutes. That's when I realized this car had the same airport rental car inspection sticker on the front driver's-side windshield like Kevin had on his rental car. I couldn't see which rental car company owned the car, but at least now I knew it was a rental. I was also aware the car had been picked up from the airport and whoever was driving it must have flown in from out of town, just like Kevin.

I swear, every word Ty uttered from her mouth seemed to be coming to fruition. I just wish she would've known who Kevin was talking to and what they had planned. Well, whoever it is, they won't come in here that easy, because I'm going to put up a hell of a fight, guaranteed.

Still reeling from the earlier unpleasant car, I couldn't motivate myself to get back to working on finding more leads on exotic cars. In fact, the only thing I wanted at this point was for Neil to come through with my firearm. So I grabbed my cell phone and dialed his number.

"Hello," he answered on the second ring.

"Hi, Neil, this is Ava. Is this a good time for us to talk?"

"Yes, sure. What's up?"

"I know you said that you'd call me, but something just happened and I'm gonna need that merchandise sooner than later."

"What happened?" he inquired.

"I caught someone through my surveillance cameras parked outside my home not too long ago, and when I walked down my driveway to confront them, they sped off," I explained.

"You know that was dangerous," Neil pointed out.

"Yes, I know. But what else was I supposed to do?"

"Call the cops."

"Yeah, I thought about it, but I didn't want to risk them leaving before the cops got here, so I tried to do it my way."

"And did your way work?"

"No."

"Exactly."

Frustrated with his response, I exhaled. "How much longer do I have to wait for my order to be filled?"

"I was getting ready to go and pick it up in within the next hour."

"Great! Could you meet me immediately thereafter?"

"About that, I would prefer you meet me at my place to pick it up."

"I don't know about that, Neil."

"Well, I can come to your place, because meeting in a public place with an unregistered firearm isn't how I do business."

I mulled over what he said for a moment and then I agreed to meet him at his home. "Okay, text me your address and I'll see you soon."

"I'm gonna text you my gate code, too," he mentioned.

"Thanks," I replied, and then we ended the call.

When the time came for me to head to Neil's place, I instructed Paulina to keep her eyes and ears open because I was about to run out for a moment. As I was leaving, I asked her if she had gotten in touch with her family yet. She said that she'd called and left a message, and was waiting for them to call her back.

The drive to Neil's neighborhood only took twenty-five minutes. Immediately after I drove up to the gated community, I pulled up next to the metal box and punched in the code he had texted me. The gates swung open, revealing a well-manicured neighborhood lined with town houses. I drove through the gate, admiring the neat lawns and the sense of orderliness the place exuded. After a few minutes I found Neil's town house. It was a sleek, modern structure with a brick facade and large windows. I parked my car and walked up the short driveway to his front door. I rang the doorbell and after several minutes the door opened.

Neil appeared with a smile on his face. "Hello, Ava!" he exclaimed enthusiastically.

I smiled back. "Hello, Neil," I said as he stepped aside so I could enter the foyer of his home.

When he began to close the door behind us, I took a few more steps forward and couldn't help but notice how impeccably clean and stylish his place was. The living room was a mix of leather and glass, with abstract art pieces adorning the walls and a large flat-screen TV mounted above a modern fireplace.

"Nice place," I commented, genuinely impressed.

"Thanks," he said, walking up behind me. "Can I get you something to drink? Water, coffee?"

"No, I'm good. I don't plan on staying long."

"Sure, no problem. Follow me, I've got your merchandise in my office."

As instructed, I followed Neil through his bachelor pad, still admiring the décor. His office was no different, with a large mahogany desk, a high-backed leather chair, and shelves lined with books and awards. He walked over to a locked cabinet and pulled out a small padded gun case. He placed it on the desk and opened it, revealing a brand-new 9mm Glock.

"Here it is," he said, stepping back so I could get a closer look.

My eyes lit up as I picked up the gun, feeling the weight of it in my hand. "Oh, my God! I love it!" I said, inspecting it closely.

Neil nodded. "It's one of the best out there, reliable and easy to handle. Let me show you a few things."

He carefully took the gun from my hand and showed me how to load the magazine, insert it into the gun, and how to switch the safety on and off. I watched politely, even though I was already familiar with the process.

"You probably know all this already," he said with a grin, "but it never hurts to go over the basics."

I nodded. "I appreciate it. Really."

After he did his brief tutorial, he handed the gun back to me, and I gently loaded the magazine and flicked the safety on, proving my familiarity with the weapon.

"You got it," he said, impressed.

"I already told you that I knew how to operate it," I reminded him while placing the gun back in the case. "I'll take good care of it. I promise."

"I'm sure you will. But just remember, you didn't get it from me," he said, his tone turning serious. "Promise me that, Ava."

"I promise," I said firmly, meeting his eyes. "No one will know where I got it from."

Neil seemed satisfied with that. He helped me close the gun case and then he picked it up and handed it to me. "Good. Stay safe, Ava."

Before I took the case from his hand, I remembered that I wanted to show him the camera footage from my home. "Wait, let me show you something," I said, grabbing my cell phone from my purse. "Look at this," I added, after opening the video app to the surveillance cameras installed in my home. I browsed through the video from earlier, and when I found the correct time stamp of the car, I handed the phone to Neil.

Neil stood there with the phone in his hand and watched as my video showed a dark car, with heavily tinted windows, slowly rolling up outside my house and park. It idled for about twenty to thirty minutes before I, in the video, exited my home and walked to my mailbox, only to turn around and approach the car a little bit later. As I soon got close to it, the car sped off. The video was shaky, but it clearly captured the vehicle's evasive behavior.

"Wow! That's not good," Neil commented as he handed my phone back to me.

"That's not all," I said, taking the phone back, switching to my photos file, and showing Neil a clear picture of the car's license plate. "I took this right before the person drove off."

Neil's brow furrowed as he studied the picture. "Do you know whose car this is?"

"No, I don't," I said, my voice tinged with frustration. "But I do know that it's a rental from the airport." I became a little more upbeat.

Neil looked at me, concern etched on his face. "Ava, this is serious. You might need to call the cops. This could be someone dangerous."

I sighed heavily, and then I slumped my shoulders. “I know. I should. But . . .”

“But what?” Neil pressed gently.

“I just have this feeling,” I said, my voice dropping, “like calling the cops will only make things worse. I can’t explain it, but something tells me to handle this on my own.”

Neil shook his head. “Ava, that’s not a good idea. You have to think about your safety. This is beyond what you can handle alone. You’ve got kids to protect.”

“I know,” I said softly. “But I also know that sometimes the police can make things more complicated. I’ll keep this evidence safe, and if things get worse, I promise I’ll go to them.”

Neil sighed, clearly unhappy with my decision. “At least let me help you. I can keep an eye on things, maybe do some digging. I’ve got connections that might be able to find out who rented that car from the airport.”

I looked at him gratefully. “Thank you, Neil. That would be great,” I said as I stuffed my cell phone back into my purse. A few seconds later, I grabbed the gun case in my hand. When I was about to turn and leave, Neil reminded me that he had a box of bullets for me. “Hey, don’t forget these,” he said as he grabbed the bag from the top drawer of his desk.

I took the bullets from his hand and stuffed them in my purse.

“Please be careful. Remember, I don’t know where you live, so it’s not like I can run over there if something happens,” he stated once again.

“I promise that I will,” I assured him.

“And will you also promise me that if things get out of control, you’ll call the cops?”

“Yes, I promise,” I said, though a part of me doubted that I would follow through. In this situation, I knew that I needed to handle this on my own terms because there’s a lot at stake.

As I was leaving Neil's town house, feelings of excitement and trepidation consumed me. I couldn't shake the feeling of unease that had settled over me. I realized Neil was right, but I also knew that involving the authorities right now might bring more trouble than it solved. I now had a firearm, which was a symbol of the lengths I would go to protect my family and me. Believe me, I would secure the safety of everyone I love, and if that meant killing someone before they killed me, then that's what was going to happen.

Neil waved me off as I exited his driveway. As I drove out of his gated community, I felt a renewed sense of determination and I was ready for whatever came next.

I couldn't believe how quickly nightfall came as I navigated the winding roads leading away from Neil's home. I gripped the steering wheel tightly as I drove down the dark streets of Houston. My eyes darted to the side mirrors and then the rearview mirror every few seconds. I could feel a knot of anxiety tightening in my chest and a feeling came over me that someone might be following me. The headlights of the occasional car passing by caused my heart to race, but I eventually breathed a small sigh of relief each time they continued on their way without turning to follow me.

The night was pitch black, the only light coming from the soft glow of my dashboard and the sparse streetlights along the way. My mind was a whirlwind of thoughts, but I forced myself to focus on the task at hand. I used my GPS and mixed in several unnecessary turns to ensure no one was trailing me. I even looped around my neighborhood twice, my eyes scanning for any suspicious figures or vehicles lurking in the shadows. When I realized that things looked normal, I proceeded to go home.

When I finally approached my house, I slowed down, peering into the darkness for any signs of movement. My large property, with its long driveway and secluded surroundings, offered privacy, but also added to my sense of vulnerability. So, as I turned to enter my driveway, I dialed Paulina's cell phone number and prayed that she answered it. My heart pounded while I listened to the phone ring. It had been several hours since I last spoke to her, so I needed to know that she was in the home, safe and sound, before I entered the residence. She finally answered after the third ring.

"Paulina, are you in the house? Is everything okay?" I asked, my voice a mixture of urgency and relief.

"Yes, ma'am, I'm inside. Everything is fine here," she replied, her tone calm and composed.

"Okay, well, I'm about to drive into the garage. Meet me at the door of the mudroom," I instructed.

"All right, I will be right there."

Immediately after I hung up, I used the remote control, which was snapped onto my sun visor, and watched the garage door slowly rise. When the door rose high enough for my SUV to drive inside, I proceeded forward. Right after I put my car in park, I pressed the button again to close the garage door behind me. And only after it had closed completely, I turned off the engine. A couple seconds later, the door to the mudroom opened, and Paulina stood there, holding it ajar. Her presence was a comforting sight. I smiled, grabbed my purse with one hand, the gun case with the other, and hopped out of the car.

"Thank you, Paulina," I said, giving her a grateful smile as I walked toward the door.

"It's no problem, ma'am. I'm glad you're back home and that you're safe," Paulina replied, returning the smile.

The moment I entered my house, I felt its warmth enveloping me. I felt safe. After I closed the door behind me and locked it, the fear of the unknown, which had gripped me earlier, slowly began to ebb away. Maybe it had something to do with the gun I was carrying in this case, or the fact that Neil had offered to find out who had rented the black car. Whatever the cause was, it felt good. And finally I felt like I was back in control.

As I walked by Paulina, I saw her stare at the gun case, but she didn't ask what it was. That was what I liked the most about Paulina. She knew how to mind her own business, and she allowed me to be me, no matter what. The fact that she trusted me meant the world to me, too, which was why I've had her in my life for as long as I have. She had become like a mother to me, as well as my confidante. I could never replace her. She was my ride or die—for life.

"Want me to make you some coffee or tea?"

"No, I'm just gonna go to my bedroom and lie down," I told her.

"Talked to the kids today?"

"You know what? I haven't. And I told Kevin to call me when they got up this morning. I guess with everything that happened earlier, it kind of threw me off track."

"Yeah, that was kind of weird. While you were gone, I kept my eyes open the entire time."

"So you never saw the car come back?"

"No, ma'am, it didn't return."

"Well, let's make sure the windows and doors are locked before we go to bed."

"I've already done that, but I'll check again."

"Thank you, because you know we can't be too careful."

"I understand, ma'am," Paulina agreed.

I nodded, feeling a profound sense of gratitude for Paulina's unwavering support for me. As she walked in the opposite direction, to do the rounds of the house, I smiled at her, and then I headed toward the staircase to go to my bedroom. I wanted to reacquaint myself with my new purchase, just so I could get a better feel for it.

CHAPTER 20

Lacey

It was Saturday night and we finally touched down in the city of Houston, Texas. After Maceo and I settled into our Airbnb, I called my mercenary to check in and get an update. Nasir was a Somalian immigrant and only went under a first-name basis. Maceo and I have been using his services for a few years now. He came highly recommended to us when we needed someone who owed us a lot of money eliminated, but they were very hard to find. Nasir found our deserter underground and made him disappear forever. What I like most about how Nasir conducts his business is none of his murders have ever been linked back to us.

"Hey, my guy, are things ready on your end?" I didn't hesitate to ask as soon as he answered.

"Well, I had a mishap earlier, but I don't think it's gonna cause a problem."

"What happened?"

"I went to the address you gave me to stake out the place and take some video footage so I could better plan how I'm gonna proceed. After parking my vehicle and scoping out the place, the target came outside and walked down the driveway to her mailbox. She looked inside of it and then turned around and caught a glimpse of the rental car I was driving. Then she started walking toward the car."

"What did you do?"

"I drove off."

"How close to the car did she get? Did she get a look at you?"

"No, the tint on the windows are really dark, so I'm sure she didn't see me."

"Okay, great. We *can't* have any *screwups,*" I stressed. "So, did you get whatever you needed while you were out there?"

"I got what I needed for today. But I will be making another visit out there right before the sun comes up."

"Nasir, you know I don't say this often, but *please* don't screw this up."

"I won't. I promise."

"I'm gonna hold you to that," I made clear, and then I said, "Has she changed her look from the photo I sent you of her?"

"No, she looks the same. She hasn't changed a thing."

"Good. That's great."

"You guys are still coming along for the ride, correct?"

"Yes, we are. And I know this is something you usually don't allow your clients to do, but in this case I have to be there. There are some things that I need to retrieve from her place myself and I will not trust anyone else to do it," I said with finality.

"Perfectly understood."

"So, what time are we getting the show on the road?"

"I would like to get her when she's not inside the home. From the looks of things, she has a lot of security cameras installed outside her home and it appears that it may be connected to a home security system provider. If that's the case, that provider will dispatch the cops if she hits the alarm switch on us. So, again, our best bet will be to ambush her while she's walking into her home," he suggested.

"Well, then that's what we'll do," I agreed. "Do you have a time in mind?"

"No, but it will be after nightfall."

"But what if she doesn't come out after dark?"

"You said that her husband was in town, right?"

"Yes."

"Problem solved. Worst-case scenario, we'll get him to lure her out of the house."

"All right, let's do it," I confirmed.

"Okay, I'll touch base with you tomorrow before I make a move."

"Sounds good," I told him.

"Oh, and one last thing, I've decided not to bring my guys into this."

"Why the sudden change?" I asked Nasir. I was starting to get concerned.

"Because I don't want to waste any of my manpower. After I saw my target in person, I knew that I wasn't going to need any help. Trust me, she's gonna be easy and I'll be in and out."

I sighed heavily and then said, "Okay, you know best."

"All right, then. If anything changes, I will give you a call."

"Please do," I stated, and then we ended the call.

Worried about the encounter Nasir had with Ava, and the fact that he switched up the plan, I decided to check in with Kevin to see if he had heard anything from Ava about the incident that transpired earlier. When he answered, Kevin told me that he had just returned from seeing a movie with his kids.

"Got a moment?" I asked him.

"Yeah, sure, hold on a minute," he said, and then I heard him moving around. "Hey, kids, give me a second. I'm gonna step outside on the balcony and take this call really quick, okay?"

"Okay," I heard his kids say in unison.

A few seconds later, I heard more movement and then Kevin said, “Okay, you’ve got my undivided attention.”

“Great. I just wanna let you know that we’re here, so I’m just checking in to see if anything has changed since we last spoke?”

“No, not to my knowledge,” Kevin said, and then he fell silent.

“Well, I just got off the phone with my guy and he said that he went out to Ava’s place to scope it out, and while he was sitting in his car, she came outside and approached his car. Before she could get close enough, he pulled away. So, has she mentioned anything to you about it?”

“When did this happen?”

“It happened today.”

“Well, I haven’t spoken with her today. But I talked to her last night because she wanted to say good night to the kids. But before we hung up, she asked me if she could hang out with me and the kids today.”

“And what did you say?”

“I told her I’d let her know. But if you wanna know my thoughts, since we’ve been going through the divorce, she hasn’t wanted to talk to me, much less be around me. So I found it odd that she would even ask.”

“Maybe she just wants to keep an eye on the kids.”

“Maybe.”

“Well, I’ll tell you what, if she happens to mention it again, you let me know.”

“Okay, I can do that. But is everything still a go?”

“Yes, it is. And now that I think about it, I may need you to do a small job for me, so keep your phone on.”

“For what?”

“I’ll let you know when the time is right.”

Kevin hesitated, but then he said okay. I sensed that he didn’t like the idea of me wanting him to get his hands dirty, but I’m afraid that he didn’t have a say in this matter. What I say goes, end of story.

"One last thing," I changed the subject. "When you were at Ava's home, did you see Nick's computer lying around anywhere?"

"Well, I only spent time in the media room, but I had to walk through the living room and the kitchen to get there, and I didn't see it."

"Do you know where she could be hiding it?"

"If I know her, it's probably somewhere in her bedroom."

I sighed. "All right. What about the money?"

"What about it?"

"What bank do you think she's hiding it in?"

Kevin hesitated, considering the possibility. "Ava's a smart woman, so I'm not sure. I mean, we both bank at Wells Fargo, as well as Chase, but I don't think she'll put it in either of those accounts."

"Well, we've gotta find out where that money is before she tries to move it offshore."

"It wouldn't surprise me if she already has. Her housekeeper is a Mexican immigrant, so she could've used her to move it."

"Good to know. But if you find out otherwise, hit me up."

"Will do," Kevin said before ending the call.

After hanging up with Kevin, I looked over at my husband and said, "Think he's holding back on us and knows more than what he's telling me?"

"It didn't sound like it."

"Well, he better not be," I hissed.

"We're still getting rid of him, too, right?"

"Absolutely. Everyone must go," I said with finality.

CHAPTER 21

Kevin

LACEY'S CALL REALLY SERVED AS A REALITY CHECK. I STOOD STARING at my phone, with my mind racing all over the place. I mean, was the plan to murder Ava about to really happen? The weight of their plan was beginning to press heavily on my shoulders, making them feel super tense. What could they possibly want me to do? I sure didn't like the sound of it, and it definitely left a bad taste in my mouth, which led me to call Ava to see where her mind was. I knew that as soon as I talked to her, I'd be able to tell if she was spooked about something and if she was taking action behind the scenes.

I dialed her cell phone number. It rang four times before she answered.

"Hello," she said. It sounded as if she was asleep.

"Hey, did I catch you at a bad time?" I asked.

"No, what's up? Where are the kids?" she replied.

"They're lying down watching TV."

"I thought you would've called me earlier so that I could talk to them."

"We got up this morning and started our day early, so it slipped my mind," I explained while listening to the tone of her voice.

"What did you guys do today?"

"We had breakfast at the hotel, and then I took them to a Major League Baseball game. They loved it!"

"That's nice. So, what do you guys have planned for tomorrow?" She continued to probe me with questions.

"I was thinking about taking them to the zoo. Then maybe take them to the mall and do a little shopping. Little Kevin was telling me earlier that he wanted the New Balance sneakers that just came out."

"Yeah, he did tell me about those," Ava said. "Just don't go and buy them a whole bunch of things they really don't need. They've got enough stuff as it is."

I chuckled. "I won't," I assured her. "So, how are you? What did you do today?" I changed the subject, hoping she'd let down her guard and talk about anything that might have happened earlier.

"Nothing much. Ran a couple of errands and came back home. I was hoping you were going to call, so I could hang out with you guys, but when you didn't, I found a few things to do around the house."

"How are you feeling?"

"How should I feel?"

"I don't know . . ." I started to say. It was becoming apparent that she wasn't going to fill me in on anything out of the ordinary that might have happened today, such as the car incident Lacey told me about.

Then I pretended to associate the question with the fact that she might have felt lonely because she wasn't with the kids. "When you asked if you could hang out with us, you sounded like you were lonely. That's why I asked how you were feeling," I finally said, even though I was lying.

"Oh no, I'm not lonely. I only asked because it felt kind of weird with them not being here and I was missing them. That's all."

"That makes sense."

"Mind if I say good night to the kids before we hang up?" she asked. Her voice was so calm and meek. I honestly couldn't believe how nice she was being.

"Yeah, sure," I said, and then I yelled the kids' names as I walked back into the room where they were. After I told them that their mom wanted to say good night, Kamryn grabbed the phone first. "Good night, Mommy! I love you," she said after I pressed the button for the speakerphone.

"I love you, too, baby girl. Are you enjoying yourself with your dad?" Ava asked her.

"Yes," Kamryn replied.

"You're not eating too much, are you?"

"Nope."

"Okay, good. Continue to have fun and I'll see you soon," Ava said.

"Okay," Kamryn said, and then she handed the phone back to me. I held out my cell phone and told Little Kevin to come and say good night to his mother. He took the phone from me. "Hey, Mom," he said.

"Hey, baby. You good?"

"Yes, ma'am."

"How was your day?"

"It was fun. We went to see the Houston Astros play the Detroit Tigers, and the Astros won," Little Kevin replied with excitement. "Dad bought us jerseys, too," he added.

"Cool. Well, I'm glad you enjoyed yourself."

"Yeah, I had a good time. I think we're going to the zoo tomorrow."

"Your dad told me. So you go ahead and get you some rest and I will talk to you guys tomorrow," Ava told him.

"Okay. I love you," Little Kevin said.

"Love you, too, baby," Ava replied.

After they said their goodbyes, I grabbed my cell phone back from Little Kevin and said, "So, what are you getting ready to do now?"

"I'm about to lie down and get some rest," she responded.

"What's on your agenda for tomorrow?" I continued to probe, trying to gauge her temperature.

"Not sure yet. But I will find something to do," she told me, her tone still the same from when she first answered the phone.

"Well, I'm not gonna hold you up any longer. Get some rest and we'll talk to you tomorrow."

"All right," she said, and then we ended the call.

After I shoved my cell phone down in my pocket, I thought about how closed off Ava was during our conversation. I couldn't help but think that she was definitely hiding something from me. I didn't know what was going on with her behind the scenes. I couldn't allow her to screw up the plan to get rid of her. Eliminating her was the common goal for everyone, and Lacey and I weren't going to let her mess that up. I needed my money, and Lacey wanted back everything that belonged to Nick, and one way or another, we were going to get it.

As I observed the kids watching TV, I realized I hadn't spoken with Ty all day. The odd thing was that she hadn't called me, either. I had no missed calls or text messages from her, so I knew she was upset with me, maybe livid at this point. I knew that I needed to call and check in; if I didn't, I probably wouldn't have a house to go to when it was time for me to fly back to Virginia.

I paced back and forth, the faint hum of the air conditioner doing little to soothe my nerves. I sighed deeply, steeling myself for the inevitable argument, as I finally bit the bullet and dialed her number.

The phone rang—once, twice, three times. Each ring felt like a tick of a countdown to an explosion of epic proportions. Finally she answered, in a cold and dismissive voice.

"What do you want, Kevin?" Her tone was icy, devoid of warmth.

No "hello"; no "how was your day?" It was just an abrupt question that felt like a slap in the face. "Come on, Ty, let's not do this," I began, trying to keep my voice calm and measured.

"Do what?" she snapped back.

"Start off the conversation like this. Now, I know it's late, but I just wanted to call and check in on you and the baby," I told her.

Ty let out a sharp, derisive laugh. "Oh, now you want to check in? You've gone all day without calling me, Kevin. Not one single call. But now you wanna call? Do you even care what goes on here?" she roared.

"I'm sorry, Ty. Today was a really hectic day. I got caught up with my kids, and it slipped my mind," I admitted.

"Calling me slipped your mind, huh?" Her voice was rising now, the anger within her started raging out. "So your kids *there* are more important than the baby you have *here*?"

"No, I'm not saying that."

"Well, you're acting like it." Her voice screeched through the phone. "Do you have any idea what it's like to be here all day long with a baby who won't stop crying? But you don't care, because you're more worried about your other kids than you are about me and your daughter."

"Trust me, it's not like that, and I'm sorry. And I promise that it won't ever happen again," I said, feeling my patience fray.

"Yeah, right. I'll believe it when I see it," she replied, falling silent right after. But then a few seconds later, she blurted out, "It wouldn't surprise me if you've been sniffing up Ava's ass and that's the real reason why you haven't had the time to call me all day."

"No, that's not true at all. I haven't spent any time with her.

I've been hanging out with my kids, while she's been doing her thing. We have not hung out once since I've been here."

"Don't lie to me, Kevin."

"I swear, *I'm not.* As a matter of fact, the last time we really had a conversation was when I told her that I wanted my part of the ransom money back. I told her that she had until the time I leave to get it to me."

"And what did she say?" Ty wanted to know. I could tell then that she was coming around just a little bit.

"She said okay. But I could tell she was irritated by me asking for it."

"Think she'll give it to you?"

"She has no choice. It's rightfully mine."

"Think she has it?"

"Of course, she does. You should see the house she lives in now. It's freaking massive. I know she paid almost a million dollars for it. Not to mention she's now driving a brand-new Bentley truck, and that thing had to be every bit of two hundred fifty thousand dollars, and that's one on the low end. So, trust me, she is swimming in money."

"What if she spent all the money up on that stuff?"

"She hasn't."

"Well, I hope for your sake you're right."

"I am, believe me."

"Where are your kids now?" she asked.

"They're watching TV."

"I guess we all are."

"What are you watching?" I wanted to know.

"The movie *Zero Dark Thirty.*"

"Oh yeah, I like that movie."

"So, what time are you going to bed?" she queried.

"Right after I get off the phone with you."

"Well, go ahead and get you some sleep. Just call me in the morning."

"Absolutely. And kiss my baby for me."

"Already done."

"I love you," I told her.

"I love you, too," she acknowledged, and then we blew each other a kiss over the phone. Immediately thereafter, we ended the call.

CHAPTER 22

Lacey

PEOPLE OUTSIDE OF MY CIRCLE WOULD CALL ME EVIL, WHILE MY family and friends would say I was a loving and loyal person. In my opinion I would consider myself to be a no-nonsense, shrewd businesswoman. I know when to use my heart in situations and when to use my brain. Today I'm using my brain, and it's telling me to do what's necessary to avenge my brother's death, and that's what I shall do. If that means taking everyone's life that could interfere with that, then that's going to be done.

Since today is the day that Ava and I are going to come face-to-face before she takes her last breath, Maceo and I decided to leave our hotel and go to a nearby café. I wanted a change of scenery and a little bit of normalcy.

We arrived at a quaint, dimly lit café a few blocks up the street. The place was nearly empty, except for a few early risers nursing their coffees and Sunday newspapers. I chose a secluded corner booth. After we sat down, I scanned the room once more, making sure we were far enough away from prying eyes and ears.

Before Maceo and I could start talking, the waitress greeted us with two menus and placed them down on the table in front of us; then she asked if we preferred coffee or tea. We opted for hot tea, so she left our table and immediately returned with two tea bags, two cups of hot water, and a small bowl of lemons.

"The sugar is right there," she said, pointing toward the end of our table.

"Thank you," I said.

"Let me know when you guys are ready to order," she added.

"This will be good for now," I told her.

"Well, let me know if you change your mind."

"Will do," I assured her.

As soon as the waitress walked away from the table, Maceo said, "Think we're ready?"

Not sure what Maceo was trying to say, I looked at him sideways, squinting my eyes and wondered what he meant by that question. "What do you mean?" I asked. I needed some clarity before I answered his question as I opened the tea bag and dropped it into my cup of hot water.

"I know Nasir is a certified killer, but the fact that he decided to do this job alone concerns me," Maceo pointed out.

"He's not gonna be alone. We're gonna be there with him."

"I know that, but you and I both know that Ava is not your average girl. She's a very clever and calculating woman. And you and I know for a fact that if she ever gets wind of what's coming her way, she's going to take some kind of quick action. It wouldn't surprise me if she hired some protection. You heard what Nasir said—she has security cameras all around her home."

"Come on now, who will she hire? I'm sure she doesn't know anyone in Houston. She hasn't been here that long," I disagreed.

"Look, we're talking about Ava. How many years did Nick have her underneath his wing before she left him for that chump-ass buster, Kevin?"

I sat there and thought for a moment. Before I could utter a word, Maceo said, "He groomed her to be the woman she is today. He taught her how to steal cars, how to evade the cops in a high-speed chase, how to shoot firearms, take them apart and put them back together. He basically created a mercenary, and at the time he didn't realize that she was going to use what he taught her to take him out."

"Believe me, she caught him off guard, because I know my brother. If he had the slightest idea about what she was going to do, he would've put a slug in her head in the blink of an eye," I said adamantly as I stirred the sugar I had just poured inside my tea.

"I'm not disputing that." Maceo nodded, his expression grim. Then he took a sip of his tea, the steam rising between us like a silent veil. "And in knowing that, we're gonna have to go in there with our guns out and blazing. We can't mess this up, in no way, shape, form, or fashion."

I set my spoon down, my eyes sharp and focused. "We're all professionals and it's gonna be three of us. It was only Nick by himself, so this is going to be a cake walk. Wait and see," I said confidently.

Maceo took another sip from his teacup and then glanced around the café. When he looked back in my direction, I said, "Are you having second thoughts?"

"No, I'm not. I just don't want any of us to underestimate her. She has those security cameras around her house for a reason," Maceo made clear.

"Ava got those cameras because she stole my brother's fucking money, and she knew that one day we were going to find out and come looking for her ass," I growled while gritting my teeth. Just the thought of that bitch robbing my brother, immediately after taking his life, made me see red. I couldn't wait until I had my day with her. I was surely going to make her pay.

"Well, then, first things first. We're gonna have to disable the cameras."

"Nasir is going to take care of that," I reminded him.

"We're gonna also have to make sure that none of her neighbors are up, hanging outside their houses or looking out their windows, either. So, if we've gotta go in her house in the middle of the night, then that's what we've got to do."

"Let's just let Nasir handle all of that. Once he takes care of that part, then we can do our part," I stated. At this point I thought Maceo was overthinking this whole thing. He was also giving Ava more credit than she deserved. Granted, she wasn't your average housewife. In fact, she wore many hats. Because of my brother, she had been trained and equipped to do a lot of things. Protecting herself and those around her was one of them, so Maceo was right, we couldn't underestimate her. But, right now, my ego won't allow me to give her the credit she has earned over the years. The anger, rage, and discontent I had in my heart for her overshadowed what skills and expertise she possessed.

Unfortunately for her, I just wanted her dead. End of story.

"Think we should take a drive by her house while it's still early. You know, get a look at it for ourselves?" Maceo suggested.

"It wouldn't hurt. But we're gonna have to be discreet," I stated.

"Well, let's do it," Maceo insisted after taking another sip of tea.

Before I could utter another word, he took ten bucks from his pocket, tossed it on the table, and stood up.

I looked up at him. "You mean *now*?" I asked.

"Yes, now," he replied.

Instead of taking another sip of my tea, I left it there and stood up from the table, too. We exited the café a few minutes later.

Maceo and I climbed into our rental car and then he typed Ava's home address into the map app on his cell phone. After we got the directions loaded to his phone, I put the car in drive and headed that way. From where the café was located, we only had a twenty-minute drive. Before we knew it, we had arrived in her swanky community. I gripped the steering wheel so tightly, my knuckles turned white. The leather creaked underneath my fingers as my eyes took in Ava's new neighborhood. A storm of rage began to brew inside of me. Maceo sat next to me, his gaze flicking between me and the road ahead.

As we drove through this upscale community, my eyes darted from one opulent home to the next. Each mini mansion we passed only served to deepen the bitterness that clawed at my heart. "Look at this place," I uttered, my voice dripping with envy. "All of this, at my brother's expense."

Maceo glanced at me, his expression unreadable. "Stay focused, Lacey. We have a job to do."

"I know, I know," I said, my eyes narrowing as we passed by another palatial home. Then we turned a corner and Ava's house came into view. The driveway seemed to stretch on forever, leading up to a ginormous home that loomed imposingly, with a lot of land surrounding it. The house was a testament to Ava's ill-gotten gains—every brick, every window, a symbol of the life she'd stolen from my brother. Looking at this massive property made my blood boil, and a seething rage bubbled up from the pit of my stomach and started spreading through my veins like wildfire. I swear, I wanted to drive straight up the driveway and ram this entire front end of the car through the front door of her house and remind her who paid for it.

"So this is it?" Maceo said, breaking the silence.

I parked the rental car on the opposite side of the street as my mind raced with thoughts of revenge, anger, and jealousy. "I want to go in there right now," I hissed, my voice trembling with fury. "I want to make her suffer. I want to shoot everyone inside and make her feel the pain she caused me by taking my brother away from me."

Maceo placed a hand on my arm, his touch grounded me just enough to keep me from doing something impulsive. "We have to be smart about this, Lacey. We can't afford to make any mistakes. Remember the plan."

I took a deep breath, forcing myself to calm down. He was right, I couldn't afford to lose control now, not when we were so close. I had to be patient, and I had to follow the plan, even if every fiber of my being screamed for immediate revenge.

"You're right," I said through gritted teeth. "But mark my words, Maceo. She will pay for what she did. I won't rest until she does," I promised myself.

I took another deep breath, my gaze never leaving Ava's home. I could feel my rage simmering just beneath the surface, but ready to explode at any moment. But for now, I knew I had to keep it in check.

"Come on, let's get out of here before she sees us and becomes suspicious," Maceo stated.

I thought about what he said, and realized that he was right, so I put the car in drive and slowly drove away. I looked back at the house through the rearview mirror and uttered the words, "We will be back, bitch!"

CHAPTER 23

Ava

I TOSSED AND TURNED ALL NIGHT LONG IN MY BED, WONDERING IF the person driving the car was outside watching my home. The thought of it gave me an eerie feeling. I swear, I wanted so badly to go outside and canvass the neighborhood, but I knew that wouldn't be the smartest thing to do. So, from time to time, I'd scan my security cameras. Once I saw that no one was lurking in the dark, I was able to lie down and close my eyes, but I wasn't able to go completely to sleep.

It seemed like the entire night dragged on slowly. It took forever for the sun to come up, but when it finally did, I slid out of bed and made my way downstairs and fixed myself a cup of tea. After I had my tea in hand, I headed back to my bedroom and retreated to the balcony attached to my bedroom so that I could get some fresh air.

I hadn't been outside on the balcony for ten minutes when my cell phone rang. I ran back into my bedroom and grabbed it from the nightstand. I glanced at the caller ID and saw it was Neil. I answered it on the fifth ring.

"Hey, Neil," I said, greeting him warmly.

"Hey, Ava, I just called because you've been on my mind all night and I wanted to check on you."

"Neil, I really appreciate that."

"Don't mention it," he replied. "So, have you noticed any strange activity going on around your house since you got back home last night?"

I frowned, thinking back on my return home. From what I remember, it had been dark and really creepy. "No, I haven't noticed anything out of the ordinary."

"That's good. But have you been keeping an eye out on your security cameras?"

"Yes, my eyes have been glued to them," I answered, feeling a surge of gratitude for his concern.

"You may wanna keep an eye out for your children, if you decide to let them play outside today," he pointed out.

"Well, right now, they're with their dad, so I don't have to worry about that."

"Wait, your husband, he's in town?" Neil asked, his voice gentle, but still probing. It was evident that he was surprised.

"Yes, he popped up on the kids and me last night," I lied as I steadied my voice. I didn't want him to know how long Kevin had been in town, since I went to him about helping me get a gun. Didn't want to cause any suspicion.

"So, where are they now?"

"They're with him at his hotel."

"How long does he plan to be in town?"

"He said until Monday."

"Does he know about the recent problem you had?"

I paused again, because I wanted to be careful of how I answered. "I hadn't had a chance to tell him. Like I said before, he popped up on us last night after he got off his flight. We didn't have long to talk because he just wanted to get the kids and take them back to his hotel. So I packed up their things and he left."

"Well, the next time you speak with your ex-husband, I think you should tell him. Maybe he could stay in town longer to make sure you guys are good," Neil suggested, his tone serious.

"Oh no. Believe me, I can handle myself. Besides, I can only take him in small doses. See, I don't know if I told you this, but he cheated on me with a woman and they had a little girl during the affair, so I'm still reeling from that."

"I'm sorry to hear that."

"No need to be sorry. The reason why I told you is that you'd understand why my attitude is this way, and why I've decided to handle my situation on my own. See, if he had the slightest inclination that me and our kids were in danger, he'd try to take them from me, and I can't have that."

"I understand perfectly."

I bit my lip as my gaze drifted to the window and watched the birds as they flew by. I wondered how my life would be if I were able to fly around as freely as them and not have a care in the world.

"Well, I'm here, if you need me. You know I have an arsenal in my possession, and I would come and be your personal bodyguard, if need be," he volunteered. His voice was very authoritative and firm.

I immediately closed my eyes, feeling the weight of Neil's words, but happy at the same time that he'd be willing to undertake such a task for me, knowing he could be putting himself in a dangerous situation. I swear, I was admiring him more and more by the minute. I mean, this man didn't know me. He had only been in my company twice; so to do this gave me a newfound respect for him. He was actually turning me on because it had been some time now since a man has stepped up to defend me. When I was married to Kevin, I didn't feel fully safe in his presence, which was why I'd go to Nick for help. Too bad he's gone now, so just maybe Neil could take that spot.

"Good to know, and I'll tell you what, I will definitely keep you in mind if anything goes down," I assured him.

"Great," he replied, a sense of relief evident in his voice. "So, what's on your agenda for today?" he wanted to know.

"Not sure yet. I may just hang around the house and declutter some of my kids' clothes," I said.

"Well, I'm gonna go and play golf for a couple of hours, but if you wanna hang out later and get a bite to eat, you know where to reach me."

"Okay, I'll keep that in mind," I said, a small smile returning to my lips. "Thank you, Neil. For everything."

"Anytime, Ava. Take care of yourself, okay?"

"I will," I promised.

CHAPTER 24

Lacey

IT WAS NINE FORTY-FIVE AT NIGHT AND I HAD BEEN WAITING FOR Nasir to call me for the past two hours, giving me the green light to meet him at Ava's place. Finally he called, but it wasn't what I wanted to hear.

"Talk to me," I said after answering the phone and then immediately putting it on speaker so that Maceo could hear the entire conversation.

"I'm not seeing any movement. I can't tell if she's inside the house or she's gone," Nasir stated.

Frustrated, I barked, "Go look in one of her downstairs windows."

"She has light and movement sensors all over her property, so when there's movement, the security cameras are instantly activated and start recording," he explained.

"So, whatcha telling me? We're not gonna be able to get into her home tonight?" I roared. I was not pleased with what Nasir was telling me. I wanted some progress, and he wasn't giving it to me.

"Can you get the husband to call her and see if she's inside?" he asked.

"Yeah, I can do that. Let me call you right back," I said, and then I abruptly disconnected the call.

"You're getting ready to call Kevin?" Maceo asked.

"Yeah," I said while dialing Kevin's cell phone number. It rang three times before he answered.

"Hello," he said, sounding like he was out of sorts.

"It's Lacey."

"What's up?"

"When was the last time you talked to Ava?"

"This morning, why?" Kevin wanted to know.

"Because my guy isn't sure if she's inside the house or not, so we're gonna need you to call her and find out where she is."

"All right, give me a second and I'll call you back," he said.

CHAPTER 25

Kevin

I SWEAR, I DREADED CALLING AVA THIS TIME OF THE NIGHT. SHE WAS a very bright woman, and she could smell bullshit from a mile away. So, before I dialed her number, I asked the kids if they wanted to talk to their mother. When they both said yes, I knew that I had a good reason to call Ava and she wouldn't get suspicious once I asked her what she was doing.

After Little Kevin and Kamryn gathered around me, I dialed Ava's cell phone. She answered on the second ring.

"Hello," she said.

"Hey, whatcha doing?" I asked.

"Just getting out of the shower and lying here in bed, watching TV. Why?"

"Because the kids want to say good night to you," I answered.

"Let me talk to them, then."

I handed Kamryn the phone after I put the call on speaker. "Hey, Mommy," she said with excitement.

"Hey, baby, whatcha doing?"

"Watching TV."

"What are you watching?"

"*The Wizard of Oz*. Daddy ordered it for us."

"Are you enjoying it?"

"Yep."

"Well, go ahead and finish watching it, while I say good night to your brother."

"Okay," Kamryn said.

"Love you."

"Love you, too," Kamryn said, and handed the phone to Little Kevin.

"Hey, Mom," Little Kevin said.

"Hey, baby, you good?" I heard Ava ask.

"Yeah, I'm good."

"Are you watching *The Wizard of Oz,* too?"

"No, I'm playing a game on my Nintendo Switch."

"Now, don't be up all night playing with that thing."

"I won't."

"Okay, let me get some rest. I've been out running around all day and I'm tired," Ava told him.

"All right," Little Kevin replied.

"Love you," Ava said.

"Love you, too," Little Kevin told her, and then they ended the call.

CHAPTER 26

Lacey

MACEO AND I HAD TO WAIT FIFTEEN MINUTES BEFORE KEVIN called us back. I was not a happy camper, either.

"What took you so damn long?" I barked.

"I couldn't make it obvious why I was really calling. So I let the kids say good night to her and that took some time," he declared.

"Where is she?"

"She's home. She said she just got out of the shower and she's about to watch a little bit of TV before going to bed."

"Is she alone?"

"You mean, is the housekeeper there?"

"Yes, her and anybody else."

"I'm sure Paulina is there, but no one else. Ava doesn't have people around her like that."

"What about a man? Is she seeing anyone new?"

"I don't think so. I mean the kids haven't mentioned anything about it."

"Okay, good. Stay by your phone," I instructed.

Kevin hesitated, but then he said, "Will do."

I disregarded Kevin's pause, and let it go and pretended that it didn't happen, and then I cleared the line. My main focus was getting Nasir back on the phone so we could deliver the news he had been waiting for me to share. I called him and gave him the information he needed.

His response, "Well, since she's inside and there to stay, then we're gonna need her husband to lure her out or at least get her to open the front door. Because if I try to walk anywhere near her home, the security sensor is going to alert her, and I know without a doubt she'll call the cops."

"Okay, stand by. I'm gonna call him back and tell him to get his ass over there."

"Roger that."

CHAPTER 27

Kevin

AFTER GETTING OFF THE PHONE WITH LACEY, A HUGE BALL OF anxiety formed inside of me and fell into the pit of my stomach. I couldn't say if it was the fact that I knew Ava was about to meet her demise or it was because Lacey told me to stand by my phone because she had some unfinished business with me. Whatever it was, I didn't have a good feeling about it either way.

I tried to calm down my nerves by grabbing and cracking open a beer from the minibar. I took a couple of sips and retreated back out to the balcony, taking a seat in one of the lounge chairs so I could get some fresh air and clear my head. The kids were sprawled out on the bed—one watching a movie, the other playing a video game—so I didn't have to worry about them interrupting me.

Halfway through my beer, my cell phone rang again. When I looked down at the caller ID, I saw it was Lacey. As much as I didn't want to answer it, I knew I had to, so I did.

"Hello," I said, feeling a huge lump form in my throat.

"Hey, I'm gonna need you to meet me in the parking lot of

the H-E-B grocery store off Fresno and Maverick Highway. It's a mile up the street from Ava's house," Lacey said, her voice coming through the line, cold and sharp.

"When?" I asked.

"Like right now."

I frowned, confusion clouding my features. "What is this about?"

"I'll explain it to you in person," Lacey replied curtly. "Just be there."

I gazed at my children, then back to my cell phone. "Well, I'm not gonna be able to come. I have my kids with me."

"Then bring them." Lacey's tone was impatient, a hint of threat laced her words.

"Come on, that's an insane idea. I can't bring my kids with me," I protested, my voice tense. "We're gonna have to do this tomorrow."

There was a pause on the other end of the line, and when Lacey spoke again, her voice was ice-cold. "Kevin, if you don't meet me, I swear I'll send someone after you and your children. *Do you understand me?*" she roared.

The words Lacey uttered made my heart skip a beat, and I immediately tightened the grip around my phone because I knew Lacey wasn't making any idle threats. She was a woman of her word. Seconds later, I glanced at Little Kevin and Kamryn, their innocent faces oblivious to the danger. I realized that I couldn't risk their safety.

"All right," I said reluctantly. "I'll be there. But I'm leaving my kids at the hotel."

"Suit yourself. But you better make it quick," Lacey warned before hanging up.

Immediately after Lacey disconnected our call, I let out a long, exasperated breath as my mind began to race. Instantly an intense level of anxiety devoured my entire body. I knew then that I needed a plan, but what kind?

I had no idea what Lacey wanted or what she was going to ask me to do. This didn't sit right with me. I did, however, know that it had something to do with Ava. I just couldn't quite figure out what it could be—and this concerned me. I figured I had done my part by telling her about Nick's murder, and then giving her Ava's home address. At this point I had done all I could. My job was complete.

I reluctantly stood up from the lounge chair and walked back into the hotel room, where my kids were. I forced a smile and said, "Hey, guys! Daddy needs to step out for a bit. But I will be right back. You two stay here and watch TV and don't open the door for anyone."

Little Kevin sat up in the bed, his eyes wide with curiosity. "Where are you going, Dad?"

"Just need to handle something really quick," I replied, trying to sound casual. "I'll be back before you know it. And if you need anything, call me. Not your mother, but me."

"Okay," Little Kevin replied.

Kamryn nodded, her attention already drifting back to the movie. Satisfied that they felt comfortable with me leaving them alone, I grabbed the rental car keys and left the room.

The drive to the address of the H-E-B felt like an eternity, especially while replaying Lacey's threat, over and over again, in my head. When I finally pulled into the parking lot, I spotted Lacey and Maceo waiting, parked back near the far end. I parked my car and got out, my heart pounding uncontrollably.

As I approached their parked car, Lacey and Maceo got out and they both leaned against the hood. After I got within arm's reach of them, I gave them a serious look, but Lacey spoke first. "I see you finally made it."

"No disrespect, but please don't ever threaten my children. You know for a fact that Nick wouldn't approve of this." I looked directly at Lacey.

Lacey chuckled. "Wait, didn't you say that my brother was the one who kidnapped your kids?"

"Yeah," I replied nonchalantly.

"Well, it sounds to me that he didn't give a fuck about them, either."

"Come on, Lacey, really?" I said, trying to defuse a flame she was trying to spark. Simultaneously I watched her husband through my peripheral vision. His face was menacing and hard lined. I could tell that he was ready to leap in my direction if he got the slightest indication that I was about to disrespect his wife.

"You set yourself up for that one," she commented with a smirk.

I rolled my eyes after realizing I wasn't gonna win this battle with her and reeled my aggression back in. I decided to take a different approach. "Can you tell me what was so important for me to come out here?"

Lacey smiled and said, "I'm glad you asked"; then she stood up from the hood of the car and walked a couple steps toward me. "In order to pull tonight's job off, we're gonna need you to get Ava to open her front door and let us in," she added.

I shot Lacey a surprised look as anxiety brimmed inside of me. "Now, how do you expect me to do that?" I asked, but at the same time not wanting to hear her answer.

"I actually don't care how you do it, but we're running out of time, so I'm gonna need you to think of something really quick."

Immediately my frustration was boiling over, and I couldn't think straight. I mean, how the hell did she think I was going to be able to get Ava to open her front door and let me into her house? Was Lacey off her rocker or something? I wanted to ask her if she was hearing herself right now, because what she said sounded downright crazy.

"Come on, you're wasting time," she said.

I could tell she was losing patience with me. My eyes narrowed. "Lacey, do you realize what you're asking me to do is damn near impossible? If I go to her house at this time of the night and ask her to open the front door, and I don't have my children with me, she's gonna become suspicious and she won't open up. In fact, she's gonna want to know where the kids are and immediately know that something is wrong. She's not stupid, Lacey, and you know it. She's gonna see right through it and call the cops," I stated.

"Well, then I suggest that you go back to the hotel, grab your kids, and bring them along," Lacey demanded.

"I'm not fucking doing that!" I barked, not realizing that I had postured myself as if I was about to go in attack mode.

Maceo quickly jumped into action. He grabbed his gun from his waist and leapt toward me. "I suggest you stand down," Maceo hissed as he pointed the barrel of the Glock directly at my forehead.

My eyes grew wide, and at that moment I saw my life flash before me. I saw my life ending, and my kids were crying at my funeral because they no longer had me or their mother. It was a grim vision, so I backed down. I took a deep breath in an attempt to calm my heart down from Maceo's intimidating presence.

Once Maceo realized that I was no longer a threat to Lacey, he took the gun away from my head and took a couple steps backward, but the atmosphere was still tense.

Lacey gave me a once-over and chuckled. "You know what, Kevin? You really got some balls! My brother always said that you were a pussy, but tonight you would've definitely proved him wrong. And you know what else? He would've been proud of how you stood up for yourself right now."

I stood there not knowing what to say. I was at a disadvantage because I was alone, and I wasn't packing a firearm like they were. I was truly outnumbered at this point, so I stood there at their mercy.

"So, what is it going to be, Kevin?" Lacey continued after looking down at her wristwatch. "You're fucking up our window of opportunity," she added, her stare hardened.

As heart-wrenching as it was, I stood there for a second, my mind racing, trying to come up with a good reason to call Ava and convince her to open up her front door this time of the night for me—without our kids in tow. I knew that whatever I said to Ava, she would see right through it, so I began to lose hope.

"Kevin, I don't like how you're stalling," Lacey pressed.

"Lacey, I'm trying to think of something plausible to say when I call her," I replied, feeling the regret that I had gotten involved in this mess. But since my children's lives were at stake, I had no choice but to do what I was told.

"I'll tell you what, call Ava and tell her that you're on your way to her house because both of the kids are sick from a stomach virus. And when you get there, you're gonna call her back so she can help you bring them inside," Maceo suggested.

"Fuck yeah! That's a good one," Lacey said with a burst of excitement. "Call her right now," she urged me, and then she curled her lips into a thin smile.

Feeling a sense of dread, I pulled my cell phone from my back pants pocket and looked at the screen for a brief second. After keying in my keypad code, my call log opened up. Before I pressed down on her number to activate the redial function, I swallowed hard as I began to gather my thoughts. I knew I couldn't mess this up or it was my life.

I dialed Ava's number reluctantly and stood there before them as it rang.

"Put it on speaker so we can hear it," Lacey ordered.

The moment Ava answered the phone, I put the call on speaker. Lacey and Maceo surrounded me, listening intently.

"Hello," she said, sounding a little groggy.

"Were you asleep?" I asked.

"I was. Why?"

"The kids are sick. And I think they may have caught a stomach virus or something," I began to say, forcing a note of urgency in my voice.

"When did this happen? I just talked to you about an hour ago, and they sounded fine," Ava replied, her voice was sharp with worry.

"Little Kevin started throwing up, literally after we hung up, and Kamryn's been complaining that her stomach hurts. So I know it's a matter of time before she starts throwing up, too," I lied, trying to sound convincing as I glanced at Lacey and Maceo, who nodded encouragingly. "I thought about taking them straight to the hospital, but then I figured it might be better if you saw them first and you could determine their level of health for yourself. And then we can figure out whether or not they really needed to go."

There was a pause at the other end of the line; then Ava's voice came back filled with both urgency and calm determination. "Where are you now?"

"I'm about ten minutes away," I answered, glancing at Lacey and Maceo for confirmation. They nodded again, satisfied with my answer.

"Okay," Ava said, her tone a mix of concern and readiness. "Call me when you're pulling into the driveway."

"Okay, I will," I promised. "See you in a minute."

I ended the call and looked at Lacey and Maceo, who exchanged menacing smiles. "It's done," I said, my voice hollow.

"Good job," Lacey replied, her eyes cold. And then she turned her attention toward Maceo. "Call Nasir and tell him to come to us because he's going to hop in the car and drive back in with us."

"I'm on it," Maceo said, and then he pulled out his cell phone. I watched him dial the person Lacey instructed him to call; then a few seconds later, I heard him say, "Hey, there's a change of plans. Meet Lacey and me in the H-E-B grocery store parking lot. It's a mile from where you are." I couldn't hear what the other party was saying, but I'm sure he said okay, because Maceo disconnected the call immediately thereafter.

"What did he say?" Lacey didn't hesitate to ask.

"He said that he's on his way," Maceo replied.

"All right, let's get ready," Lacey said with eagerness.

I stood there with my stomach knotted up like a nautical rope. All kinds of scary scenarios popped up in my head about how tonight was going to go down. Honestly speaking, I felt this was not the way Ava's murder was supposed to be carried out. I was supposed to be at the hotel room with my kids while they did what they were going to do with Ava. Now I'm caught in the middle of this bullshit, and I don't know how this is going to end. Not to mention, I haven't gotten my money from Ava yet. Would it be appropriate to ask her for the money before they kill her? And will she give it to me? Not only that, what makes them think that I want to stick around when they kill her?

I don't want to see my wife die right in front of me. I'm a vengeful type of person, but I'm not that damn fucked up. I mean, Ava does still mean something to me. Shit, we've been married for over ten years, not to mention we have two children together. So, to witness them take her out, I don't want to stick around for that. I do have a conscience, whether anyone believes it or not. Hopefully, after we get to her residence and they have her where they want her, they will let me go back to the hotel, where my kids are.

"So, are we gonna stand here and wait for him?" I blurted out, because I was feeling a bit weird and awkward.

"Well, since we're riding in your car, I guess we can start putting our things in there," Lacey spoke up.

"What kind of things do you have?" I wondered aloud.

"I'm not sure what our guy has with him, but I have a satchel of tools I figured may come in handy in case I need to break down a wall, crack open a safe, or haul a lot of shit out of her house," Lacey explained.

"Oh, okay," I said nonchalantly. Truthfully speaking, I didn't know what else to say. It felt like I was in the twilight zone, and I didn't know how I was going to get out of it.

Lacey tried to make small talk about how she couldn't wait to get this over with so that she and Maceo could get back on the plane and head home. I tried to block out all the nonsense she was saying because her voice was becoming irritating. At one point I wanted to tell her to shut up. But I knew Maceo would be on me and probably try to put me in a headlock or something, so I left well enough alone.

The guy they were waiting for finally pulled up about eight minutes later. The sound of the engine as the car slowly pulled in stopped Lacey in midsentence, and my pulse quickened as my stomach began to feel sick. After he parked his car next to the car Lacey was driving, he opened the door slowly and climbed out of it, with a small cross-shoulder bag attached to him. He also had a gun in hand, but he stuck it in his waist before he closed the car door. My eyes immediately widened as I took in the appearance of the guy.

"Glad to see you join the party," Lacey said to him.

The guy didn't crack a smile. He kept a straight face. I looked at him from head to toe. He was tall, his height adding an intimidating presence to the already-horrifying atmosphere. He moved with slow and measured steps, as if he were acting out a role in a movie. His face was an unreadable mask, motionless and devoid of any discernible emotion. I strained to see his eyes, but the darkness shrouded them, leaving only the impression of an inscrutable, predatory gaze.

His body language spoke volumes, even in the absence of words. His shoulders were broad and squared, his posture relaxed but alert. He exuded an air of confidence, a man who was utterly in control of himself and his surroundings. I could also sense the coiled power in his movements, like a panther ready to strike. It was clear that this was a man who was accustomed to violence, who had seen and done things that most people couldn't even imagine. And he gave off the impression that he was ready to kill.

At one point he looked at me from head to toe and I swallowed hard, trying to steady my nerves. Believe me, I had dealt with dangerous men like this before, but for some reason I knew this man was different. There was a cold, professional detachment about him that was more unnerving than outright aggression, and I knew instinctively this guy was not someone that I wanted to mess with.

"So you're the husband?" he asked me, his tone was low but stern. The sound sent a chill down my spine.

I nodded.

"All right, let's go," he said, and then he waited for me to make the first move.

As I started walking back toward my rental car, I realized that I had made a deal with the devil and there was no turning back.

Now as everyone followed me to the car, I couldn't shake the feeling of dread that hung over me. I thought about Ava, about the life that we had before this, and about the children we shared. I also couldn't stop thinking about the guilt that was consuming me. I honestly felt like shit. The gravity of this situation was getting the best of me, but I had to protect my children. And besides, Ava put this on herself. All she had to do was give me my part of the ransom back, when I first asked for it, and none of this would be happening.

After everyone climbed inside the backseat of my car, I powered up the engine and then I headed to Ava's place.

When I reached the familiar streets of Ava's neighborhood, my heart rate sped up quickly as her house came into view. As badly as I wanted to turn the car around, I knew that if I did, someone in the backseat would put a bullet in my head quickly—and I'm trying to walk away from this alive for my kids.

"Call her now," Lacey interrupted my thoughts the moment the car got within inches of the mailbox.

As instructed, I pulled out my cell phone and dialed her number, my hands slightly trembling. But before I could press the SEND button, the front door of Ava's house opened and the light from inside the house illuminated the entire doorway and part of the walkway in front of the home.

"Drive slowly." Lacey's instructions continued from the backseat, her voice low and calm.

Instead of responding, I did what I was told and drove at a slow pace. The palms of my hands were sweaty, while my heart felt like it wanted to leap from my chest. I heard movement in the backseat, but I didn't dare look back to see what was going on. I kept my eyes front and center to prevent myself from rubbing anyone the wrong way.

Immediately after I stopped the car, Ava shot away from the entryway of the front door and proceeded toward my car. This made Lacey very happy. "Attagirl, come on to Mommy," she said in a dark and sinister manner. It sounded almost mechanical.

"Where are they?" Ava yelled from the outside as she stood next to the passenger-side door, wearing pajamas and slippers.

As her eyes peered through the windows of the rental car for the kids, I had to admit that I instantly felt a moment of intense regret, but it was too late to turn back now.

Lacey, Nasir, and Maceo moved swiftly, and I watched, my heart breaking as the reality of my actions finally hit me. Ava's look of confusion turned to horror when she realized what was happening, but by then, it was too late.

Both of the back doors of the car swung open. Lacey and Maceo jumped out on the driver's side, while their hit man came out of the passenger side. I couldn't see Ava's facial expression after she stood straight up, but I heard her gasp. Then she attempted to turn and run, but the hit man pointed his gun at her with a silencer attached to the barrel and said, "Run, bitch, and I will shoot you in the back."

Ava heeded the threat and didn't move an inch. I sat in the car and watched as Lacey and Maceo walked around the back of the car to come face-to-face with Ava. I couldn't see anyone's faces, but I heard every word spoken.

"Never thought you'd see my face, huh?" Lacey said.

"What's going on? Why are you guys here?" Ava tried to speak calmly. She knew she was outnumbered and didn't have a fighting chance with three against one, so she stood there at their mercy.

"Kevin, get out of the car so we can all go inside the house," Lacey demanded.

I rolled down the passenger-side window and said, "But I thought my job was done after I got her to come outside?"

"Man, get your bitch ass out of the car!" Maceo roared as he stuck his arm through the passenger-side window and pointed his gun at my face.

Having Maceo point his gun at me for the second time in less than thirty minutes gave me a clear sign that he wanted to put a bullet in me really bad. So, without further hesitation, I got out and walked around the car where everyone was standing. I tried avoiding eye contact with Ava and she noticed it.

"Kevin, tell me what this is all about? Where are my children?" Ava asked.

"We will get to that as soon as we get in the house," Lacey interjected, and then seconds later, we all moved into the house.

CHAPTER 28

Lacey

"HURRY UP AND CLOSE THE DOOR BEFORE SOMEONE SEES US," I instructed Maceo after we entered Ava's home.

After everyone piled inside of her house, I stood there for a moment and looked around. I was immediately taken aback by the sheer beauty and elegance that surrounded me. The grand foyer was adorned with a crystal chandelier, and intricately carved crown moldings lined the ceilings. The walls were adorned with beautiful artwork. The furniture was luxurious, including plush sofas and mahogany tables. And I could tell that the rugs she had on the floor were imported. They alone had to be at least forty thousand each, and I saw three of them.

Instantly a stroke of envy and rage engulfed my entire being. I remembered how she used my brother's money to acquire all of this after she murdered him. In my eyes this was blood money.

"So this is where my brother's money was spent," I commented, my voice laced with disdain.

Ava looked at me, perplexed. "Your brother's money?" Ava replied, trying to act dumbfounded.

My eyes narrowed as I stepped closer to her. "Yeah, my brother's money. Bitch, I know you stole the money from his safe. And I know you have his laptop and the millions of dollars he had in offshore accounts."

Ava's eyes widened in shock. "I don't k-know what y-you're talking about," she stammered, trying to maintain her composure.

My facial expression twisted in anger. "Don't fucking lie to me, bitch! I know the truth. Kevin told me everything. Now shut the fuck up and tell me where the housekeeper Paulina is," I ordered aggressively.

Ava immediately turned her attention toward Kevin and shot him an evil look. "You fucking traitor! So this is what it has come to? All because you couldn't get your ransom money back? You piece of shit! I can't believe that you ratted your own son out to these motherfuckers because I wouldn't give you your money back," she hissed.

Shocked by her admission, I said, "Wait a minute, what does your son have to do with this?"

"What do you mean, what does my son have to do with this? Now I'm confused," Ava replied.

I set my eyes on Kevin, hoping he'd chime in. "What about your son? What is she talking about, Kevin?"

Kevin wouldn't speak. He stayed mum and dropped his head.

I turned my attention back to Ava. "Somebody is going to tell me what your kid has to do with this situation." I wouldn't let up.

"Sounds like Kevin didn't tell us the whole story," Maceo chimed in.

"What did you tell 'em, Kevin?" Ava spoke next as she folded her arms across her chest.

"I told them *you* killed Nick, all right! You satisfied?" he spat out nervously.

Ava looked like the life was being sucked out of her after Kevin finally revealed what he'd told me. Now that the cat was out of the bag, I was ready to move on to the next step, which was to retrieve my brother's laptop and his money. After that, Nasir could have his way with her.

"You thought you were going to get away with this, didn't you?" I taunted her.

She just stood there with an emotionless face. Her eyes looked glassy.

"You ain't gotta answer me. But after tonight I'm gonna make you wish you never met me or my brother, you fucking backstabbing bitch!" I barked.

"Your fucking brother started this whole ordeal because that piece of shit standing next to you owed him money. If Kevin hadn't owed Nick money, Nick wouldn't have kidnapped my kids, and he wouldn't be dead right now," Ava barked back at me. Her face had turned red.

Without even thinking about it, I reacted by lunging at her and smacking her with the back of my hand. *Whack!* Ava stumbled backward, until she caught her balance. When she was able to stand firmly on both feet, she held her hand against her face. It looked like she was shielding the pain I had inflicted on her.

"You think I'm gonna let you just stand there and disrespect my brother like that! After all that he's done for you?"

"Look, I hate to break up this reunion, but where is the housekeeper?" Nasir asked.

"Yeah, where is your housekeeper?" I asked Ava.

"She's not here," she replied.

"She's lying," Kevin interjected.

I took a step toward Ava as I grinded my teeth together. "Lie to me again and, I promise you, I will kill your children," I threatened, my voice deadly serious.

Ava looked like her heart had stopped. I guess the thought of her children being in danger gave her a reality check. So she took a deep breath, trying to steady her nerves. "She's in her bedroom," she finally admitted, her voice barely above a whisper.

My eyes gleamed with satisfaction. "Good. Take me to her."

Then I turned my attention toward Maceo and instructed him to stay behind and watch Kevin. "Make sure he doesn't go anywhere," I said.

"But I've gotta get back to my kids. If I stay away too long, they may call the cops," Kevin complained as his voice echoed.

His voice was met with silence, heightening the level of evil that plagued the atmosphere. Before anyone had a chance to say another word, Nasir turned around and, moving with an eerie and calculated precision, lifted his 9mm Glock, with the silencer affixed to the barrel, into the air and aimed it at Kevin.

Kevin barely had time to register the danger, saying, "Wait," but his words were cut short by the soundless discharge of the weapon.

The first bullet struck Kevin in the chest. He squealed and then his body staggered backward. He immediately fell back on the sofa, and after landing on it, he looked down in disbelief at his chest. Everyone in the room could see the agony etched across his face as blood filled his mouth.

Before he could make another sound, Nasir shot him once more in the chest, and Kevin lost all motion and died instantly. All the life in him was gone, and he lay there, with his head tilted backward and his body as stiff as a board. Nasir stood there and lowered his gun. His expression was void of any emotion.

I looked at Nasir and said, "What did you do that for?"

"He was talking too much. But wait, didn't you say that he wasn't leaving out of here alive?" Nasir seemed confused as he questioned me.

"Yes, but I wanted you to wait until a little longer," I said.

Nasir hunched his shoulders. "Well, it's too late now," he said. Then he changed the subject by saying, "Now let's go and see where this housekeeper is."

"Let's go!" I happily obliged and turned around and gestured for Ava to lead the way. When I zoomed in on her, I noticed that her facial expression was a mixture of shock and fear, and then it folded into a frown after she turned her head and looked at me. She shot me a dagger of a gaze. And if eyes could kill, I would most certainly be six feet under at this very moment.

I dared Ava to confront me. "Got something you wanna say?"

She refused to say a word and just stood there.

"Come on, let's get the housekeeper and what we came here for so we can get out of here," Maceo chimed in.

"Take us to where your housekeeper is," I gave the order. Ava hesitated for a second, seeming as if she was going to retaliate. When she looked at every one of us and realized she was outnumbered, she must've come to her senses and reconsidered her position. Eventually her facial expression softened.

"Whatcha standing there for? Let's go," I snapped, losing patience with her. So, at that moment, she turned around and led the way upstairs.

CHAPTER 29

Ava

As I led these motherfuckers up my staircase, all I could think about was my husband's lifeless body lying on my sofa. I swear, as much as I hated what he had become before his murder, I couldn't believe these heathens took his life like that. And who was this fucking man?

I've known Lacey and Maceo for a very long time, and I've never seen this guy before. He was cold-blooded and unpredictable. His silent and mysterious demeanor kind of has me puzzled, too, because I can't figure out what he's thinking. I do know that these bastards are here to take Nick's things back and kill me before they leave, but I can't have that. I've got too much to live for. I can't leave my kids in this world without me. They need me. Now I don't know how, but I have to figure a way out of this.

When we got to the top of the staircase, I turned around and said, "Which one of you was in that car parked outside my house yesterday?" I asked this because I was curious, but I also wanted to get Paulina's attention by sparking up a conversation before we got to her room. Maybe if she heard me talking, she'd listen to the conversation, and once she realized that we were in danger, she'd either hide or call the cops.

Lacey spoke up first. "That's not important. Now let's keep moving."

I looked at her and rolled my eyes. She has always been a bitch and jealous of me since day one. She hated that I was with her brother, because I started running things at his shop back in Virginia. I took her spot and started handling all of Nick's day-to-day operations at the chop shop, became his best driver, and I made him an extreme amount of money. Oh, how she hated me for it, and couldn't stand being around me, which is why she relocated to California. Now I've come face-to-face with this bitch again. But this time, lucky for her, I'm at a disadvantage. But I will figure this shit out or die trying.

As we headed down the hallway to Paulina's bedroom, my heart began to pound with every step. I wanted to scream and give Paulina a warning, but I knew that it would be a bad idea, so I decided against it. Instead, I moved slowly toward her bedroom door and then I stopped suddenly. I turned around and said, "Please don't hurt her. She's an old lady who has nothing to do with this."

Lacey shoved me to the side and walked past me. She stormed toward Paulina's bedroom door and kicked it with her right foot. It flew open and my heart sank as the door hit the doorstop, which was mounted into the wall behind it. Immediately after that, she entered Paulina's room and noticed the television was on and the channel turned to Telemundo. She turned around, looked at me, and said, "She's not here."

For a moment there was only talking coming from the television, so Maceo said, "Look underneath the bed."

Lacey got down on her knees and peered underneath it. "She's not there," she announced, standing back up on her feet.

I stormed into the bedroom behind Lacey, with Maceo and the hit man in tow, and gazed around Paulina's room, hoping that she was hiding somewhere and they wouldn't be able to find her. But then the sound of running water coming from the bathroom seeped through the awkward silence.

As everyone's eyes turned in that direction, Paulina emerged, wearing a housedress, drying her hands. Suddenly her eyes widened in shock as she saw these people standing alongside me. "What's going on, ma'am? Who are these people?" she asked, her voice trembling.

I swallowed the lump that had formulated in the back of my throat and attempted to explain who everyone was, in an effort to calm her nerves a little, but Lacey cut me off in midsentence.

"Shut up," she instructed me, her eyes fixed on Paulina. "Maceo, grab the old lady and bring her with us."

Paulina looked at me, seeking reassurance, but I could only nod as I watched Maceo grab her by the arm and drag her out of the bedroom. My heart went out to Paulina as I witnessed her being forced out of the room—and I couldn't do anything to help her. The horror on her face cast a dark cloud over me, and I felt so guilty for what was happening to her.

"Let's go, bitch!" Lacey barked as she pushed me toward the door of Paulina's bedroom. I stumbled forward and started walking in the direction of my bedroom. It was only a short distance away from Paulina's room. In fact, it was only ten feet away.

"Which one is her bedroom?" Maceo asked Paulina as they moved ahead of me.

Paulina pointed at my bedroom, and immediately after she had done so, Maceo pushed her forward and instructed her to open the door. I watched Paulina open my bedroom door and then she was pushed inside. She stumbled forward and Maceo followed her inside. Lacey, the hit man, and I walked directly in behind them. Once inside, Lacey gestured impatiently. "Where is the laptop?"

I pointed to the closet, my hands trembling. "It's in there."

Lacey motioned to Maceo, who stepped forward and yanked open the closet door. He rummaged through the shelves, until he found the laptop, holding it up triumphantly.

"Got it," he said in a gruff voice.

Lacey smiled, satisfaction gleaming in her eyes. "Good, hand it to me," she said with excitement. After Maceo handed her the laptop, she opened it and noticed that you needed a password to unlock the screen. She turned to me and asked, "What's the password?"

I swallowed hard, knowing there was no easy way out of this. As I prepared to answer, I couldn't help but glance at Paulina, who stood silently a few feet away. Fear was written into her features. I realized that we were in this together now, so I knew I had to find a way to protect us.

"It's RINGSWEEP0945, all caps," I finally answered.

Lacey keyed in the password and unlocked the screen as she leveled the laptop on her left arm. She smiled instantly. I heard her click on a few more keys and then she looked back at me. "So you're pretending to be my brother negotiating another job with his connect out in Belgium, huh?" she asked.

"Say word!" Maceo exclaimed loudly as he peered over Lacey's shoulders to get a look at the laptop screen. And when he saw what Lacey saw, he looked at me and said, "You dirty bitch!"

"Yeah, she is, isn't she?" Lacey agreed. "This is a twenty-four-and-a-half-million-dollar job," Lacey said snidely as she moved toward me. "You greedy bitch! How much more money are you going to try to make off my brother's dead body?"

I stood there silently, refusing to answer her question. I knew that if I responded, it wouldn't be the answer she wanted to hear, so I remained quiet. But the fact that I refused to answer her question rubbed her the wrong way and she lunged back, hitting me across the face with an open-handed slap. *Whack!*

"Bitch, don't you hear me talking to you?" she snapped.

The blow from Lacey's slap stung my face and instinctively I pressed my hand against it, hoping that it would suppress the pain. "I didn't go looking for it, it just fell in my lap," I told her.

"The millions you've already taken from Nick just wasn't enough, huh?"

"I haven't taken any millions from him," I lied.

Lacey handed the laptop to her hit man, curled her right hand into a fist, and then she lunged a punch at me. Her hand connected to my stomach. I instantly pressed my hand against my stomach, doubled over upon impact, and coughed—or, actually, more like gagged. It felt like she had taken the wind out of me. I looked back up at Lacey and I swore I saw red flames flickering in her eyes. I saw pure hatred clouding her face.

"Stop fucking lying to me!" she spat out viciously.

As I tried to stand up straight, the pain radiating inside of me reminded me that it was too soon to make a move, so I stayed hunched over, trying to regain my strength. "I'm not lying," I finally replied.

"Fuck all that! The deal hasn't been done yet, so she hasn't gotten the money. What we should be focusing on now is where is the money she has already," Maceo brought up.

"Yeah, where did you stash *Nick's money*?" Lacey demanded.

"The only money I took was the money he had in his safe," I lied once again.

Lacey gritted her teeth and took two steps toward me. "Now, I'm gonna ask you one more time, where is my brother's money, and if you lie to me again, Maceo is going to put a bullet in Paulina's head."

Before Lacey could finish her sentence, Paulina, who had been seemingly helpless, pulled a gun from her housedress with astonishing speed and shot Maceo twice in the stomach. The room erupted in chaos as Maceo dropped the computer he had been holding, collapsing to the floor in agony.

Everyone in the room was stunned by Paulina's unexpected

move. For a moment it felt like time had stood still. But the hit man quickly regained his composure and, in slow motion, aimed his gun at Paulina. Without hesitation he released a shot and it hit her in the arm. She fell back and collapsed to the floor instantly, crying out in agony from the pain.

Seizing the moment of distraction, I dove to the floor and grabbed the gun that Paulina had dropped. As soon as I had it in my hand, I realized that it was my gun. So I aimed it at Lacey and the hit man and started firing one shot after the next. Unfortunately, they managed to dodge the bullets, barely escaping as they ran out of the room. On the way out, the hit man, reacting swiftly, returned fire with the gun he was holding. The sound of gunfire from my gun echoed throughout the house, which was a stark contrast to the previous silence.

After the hit man and Lacey disappeared from the doorway, I shot holes through the walls near the door, hoping that I'd hit one of them. When I didn't hear a groan sound, I figured they had moved farther away from my room. At that moment I hurriedly crawled across the floor, then shut my bedroom door behind them and locked it.

In a room that was now a battlefield, and an aftermath of a violent confrontation that had left Maceo dead, I found myself out of breath and out of bullets. I desperately attempted to gather my thoughts. While doing so, I quickly realized that if I wanted to come out of this thing alive, I needed to reload my clip.

I crawled back across the floor toward my desk and grabbed the box of bullets from the bottom drawer. After I reloaded the clip, I pushed it back inside the gun; then I turned my attention to Paulina, who was just a few feet away from me.

"I'm so sorry," I whispered to her as I watched her lie behind the bed in pain, suffering from a gunshot wound in her left shoulder. I quickly grabbed the pillow from my bed, snatched the pillowcase from it, and tied it around her arm. "I know that it hurts, but this will slow down the bleeding."

"Thank you, ma'am," she managed to say, her words barely audible.

"How did you know to get my gun?"

"Because I heard the commotion downstairs and since I knew where you kept it, I figured that I needed to get it." She explained.

Before I could say another word to her, all the power in the house automatically shut down. My entire house went pitch black. This meant I wasn't able to see a thing. My security system was disabled, and my fire alarm went silent. I took a deep breath, trying to steady myself and figure out my next move. The danger was far from being over, and I knew that every second counted.

As I tried to put my thoughts together, I noticed that my house was eerily quiet. It was the kind of quietness that presses on your ears and makes every small sound feel like a gunshot. I also noticed that a faint glow from the streetlight outside, at the end of my driveway, filtered through the blinds on my window. It was quite dim actually, but I made it work after I opened up the blinds wider. After I got back down on the floor, I lay down next to Paulina and tried to reassure her that everything would be fine.

"Think both of them went into the garage to turn off the breaker switches?" Paulina whispered.

"I'm not sure," I whispered back, gripping my gun tighter in my hand as my heart pounded loudly inside my chest.

Paulina's breathing was shallow, and I could feel her trembling. "What are we going to do? Wait for them to come back?" Paulina whispered once more, her voice barely audible.

I swallowed hard, trying to keep my composure. I had to stay strong for the both of us. "I've gotta figure out a way to get us out of this room," I said. "We can't stay here because they'll be back soon, and if we stay in here, they'll be able to ambush us easily," I told Paulina. Then I thought about the conversation I had with Kevin's girlfriend, Ty, and went back to the day she had warned me about how something was going down with Kevin. I just wished that I was better prepared.

"I wish I knew if my kids are safe," I said, my voice cracking with worry as my thoughts drifted to their whereabouts.

Paulina nodded, her eyes wide open with fear. "Shouldn't they be with Kevin?"

"Kevin's dead."

"What do you mean?"

"He's the one who brought these people here, Paulina. And now he's lying on the sofa in my living room dead, with two bullets in his chest," I explained.

Paralyzed by my admission, Paulina lay there, fear had worn out her face. "Mr. Frost is dead, ma'am?" she asked, wanting some clarity.

"Oh, my. So, what are we going to do?" Paulina wanted to know.

"I'm trying to figure that out right now."

"Do you think we can make it to the basement? Maybe we can hide there until help comes," she suggested.

I considered the idea. The basement was a good hiding spot, but getting there without being seen was the challenge. "I don't know about that, Paulina. The only way down there is to leave this room and head down the stairs, without being seen, and that's gonna be too risky."

"So then what do you suggest we do?"

I thought for a moment and then said, "The only way we're gonna be able to get out of here is by climbing out of this window."

"But we're on the second floor," she reminded me.

"I know," I said, realizing this was the only way she and I were going to get out of here alive.

So, as Paulina lay there on my bedroom floor, contemplating the only option we had, I noticed her breathing had become heavy and strained. The dim streetlight filtered through the blinds of my window, casting long shadows, adding to the already-tense atmosphere. I glanced at my bedroom door as my mind continued to race uncontrollably. Beyond my bedroom door Lacey and her hit man lurked in the darkness, waiting for the perfect moment to strike.

Paulina continued to add pressure to the area of her gunshot wound; her face contorted in pain. Blood seeped through her fingers, and by now, I knew my carpet had to be saturated. I knew I had to act fast or Paulina wouldn't make it. So I turned to her, my voice urgent but calm, and whispered, "We need to get out of here, Paulina. We have to get you to a hospital." I glanced at the window and then back at my bedroom door.

Paulina winced, shaking her head. "I can't, ma'am. I can barely move, and climbing out of a window . . . I'll fall for sure."

I gripped Paulina's hand and said, "Listen to me. We don't have a choice. If we stay here, they'll kill us both. The sheets from my bed—we can use them to climb down. It's the only way."

Paulina's eyes filled with fear, but she nodded slowly.

I quickly stripped the bed, knotting the sheets together to form a makeshift rope. I secured one end to the left leg of my heavy oak footboard, giving it a firm tug to ensure it would hold.

With a deep breath I helped Paulina to the window. "I'll go first and help you down," I insisted, but Paulina shook her head.

"But what if they come in here shooting, I'll be an easy target."

My heart pounded as I nodded, knowing Paulina was right. At that point I helped her out the window, guiding her hands to grip the sheets tightly. Paulina's knuckles turned white as she began her descent, her body trembling with fear and pain.

Then suddenly the bedroom door burst open with a deafening crash. I whirled around, my eyes locking onto Lacey and her hit man's dark shadows. Without hesitation I grabbed the pistol

I had on the floor next to me and began firing it. The room erupted in chaos as they returned fire, bullets whizzing past me. So I immediately ducked for cover. Before I ducked down behind my bed, I saw Lacey stagger, clutching her arm and screaming in pain. Seeing this, her hit man continued to return fire, the bullets tearing through my bedroom. I pressed myself against the floor, trying to make sure I didn't get hit.

Outside, Paulina's grip on the sheets faltered. "Ava, I can't hold on much longer!" she cried out, her voice filled with panic.

I glanced toward the window, torn between helping Paulina and defending myself. I fired a few more shots toward the door, hoping to buy myself some time. Lacey's pained screams echoed, so I knew then that I had a small window of opportunity to act quickly.

With a sudden burst of adrenaline, I jumped up toward the window. When I looked over the windowsill, I noticed Paulina was holding on to the sheets for dear life. I reached out to grab her hand and, just like that, her grip on the sheets faltered and she slipped. I heard her fall to the ground with a loud thud. I stood there in shock, but then moments later, I was brought back to reality with a gunshot that missed me by an inch, shattering what was left of my bedroom window above my head. Panic surged through me, and I immediately dove for cover behind my bed while I aimed my gun and fired until I emptied my clip. Lacey's hit man's shots shattered the mirror above my dresser, shards of glass raining down everywhere.

My heart pounded as my entire world caved in around me. I heard Lacey's labored breathing and the hit man's footsteps drawing closer. I knew I needed a plan—and fast. My eyes darted around my bedroom from where I was lying down on the floor, and I couldn't think of anything to use as a distraction to slow them down. Then it hit me that I could use my bed as a shield and then make a run for my window. However, it also dawned on me that it would be impossible to pick up my bed, so the next best thing would be to flip my mattress up on its side and use it as a shield long enough so that I could climb out the window.

So, without further ado, I mustered up all the strength I had inside, grabbed the bottom of my mattress, lifted it up, and pushed it forward. Lacey's hit man stumbled backward and fell onto the floor, giving me the split second I needed. I grabbed the comforter that was lying on my floor, laid it over the shards of glass lining my windowsill, and then I scrambled out the window, sliding down the sheets.

CHAPTER 30

Ava

MY HANDS BURNED FROM THE FRICTION, BUT I DIDN'T STOP until my feet hit the ground. When I landed, I realized that Paulina was nowhere in sight, and I immediately became alarmed. I was sure that she'd gone over to the neighbors' house to call the cops, but I wanted to make sure. I whispered her name, "Paulina," but I got no response.

My eyes darted to the shadows near the garage, where I heard muffled voices. Instantly my stomach tightened with fear. "Fuck! Lacey got Paulina," I said, my words barely audible. Guilt began to consume me, and I started fighting with myself about whether or not I should go for help or try to save her. I mean, what if I went for help and came back to find her dead? I swear that pain would haunt me for the rest of my life. Besides, she was like a mother to me, and she had nothing to do with all this mess Kevin and I created.

Even though I didn't have my gun anymore, I knew, morally, I couldn't leave her behind, so I put an *H* on my chest and began to muster up the courage to go and defend Paulina's life—no matter the cost. I took a deep breath, and then I moved slowly in the direction of the mumbling voices, staying close to the wall to remain hidden.

As I reached the edge of the garage, I peered cautiously around the corner. My heart leapt into my throat as I saw Paulina sitting on the ground, but relief washed over me when I realized that it wasn't Lacey standing over her. It was Neil, struggling to lift Paulina from the ground.

I rushed forward, my voice breaking the silence. "Paulina! Neil! Oh, my God, I'm so glad to see you both."

Neil looked up, his face etched with concern and relief. "Ava! Thank goodness you're okay. From my car I heard all the glass shattering, and when I saw your housekeeper climbing out the window, I leapt from my car and tried to help her down, but she fell before I could reach her. Then when I asked her what was going on, she told me there were intruders in your home and that you were still trapped in your bedroom."

"How did you know where I lived?" I became leery, because I was beginning to think that he could've been with Lacey and her hit man all along and had set me up.

"I put a GPS device on the case containing the gun, and that's how I knew where you lived. After you left my house, I began to worry about you and your kids' safety, which was why I decided to drive over here tonight. When I drove up and saw all the lights out in your house, while everyone else on the block had power, that concerned me, so I stopped."

"As much as I want to curse you out for putting a GPS on my gun case, I am so glad you did. There are people in my house and they're trying to kill me. If we don't hurry up and get out of here, they're gonna be out here before we know it," I told him.

Neil pulled his gun from the waist of his pants and pulled back on the chamber. "Well, I'm ready," he announced.

"*No,* we've gotta get out of here and get her to *a hospital,*" I stressed.

Neil thought about what I said for a second as he looked down at Paulina, who looked like she was on her last breath. "All right, let's get her to a hospital," he said reluctantly, and stuck his gun back inside the waist of his pants. He reached down to the ground and grabbed Paulina up.

I saw the exhaustion on her face and asked if she could walk.

"No, ma'am, I feel so weak," she answered.

"I can carry her," Neil volunteered.

"Mind if he carries you?" I asked.

"No, I don't mind at all."

At that moment Neil lifted Paulina and held her in his arms. She instantly laid her head against his chest. "You ready?" he asked me.

I took a deep breath and said, "You know we're gonna be out in the open as soon as we leave the side of my house?"

Neil thought about it and said, "Take my gun and cover me."

Without hesitation I took his gun, pulled back on the chamber, and then took a deep breath. "You ready?" I asked as the dim light of the moon cast eerie shadows on the walls of my house, making everything feel more surreal and dangerous than ever. I knew that it was either now or never, because Lacey and her hit man were inside, and the situation was about to escalate at any moment.

Neil nodded, his face carved with pain and determination as he adjusted Paulina's body weight in his arms. He gradually started walking toward his car, slowly, every step a struggle as I walked close behind him. My eyes scanned every inch of our surroundings, while I held his gun pointed in the direction of my house. I had mentally programmed myself to shoot at any movement coming from my home.

I can't lie, as we started making our way to his car, it felt like an eternity. The silence around us amplifying my fear that we would get caught up in a cross fire, because I knew that somewhere either Lacey or her hit man was lurking in the dark, waiting for me to come out of hiding so that they could pop me.

And just as fate would have it, as soon as we appeared from the side of my house, we were out in the open, with nothing shielding us as we started making our way across the open landscape of my property. I immediately heard a faint click breaking the silence, followed by the muted whisper of gunfire from a silencer. My heart skipped a beat as I saw Lacey's hit man standing in the doorway of my front door, his silhouette barely visible. His first shot hit Neil in the leg, and he instantly collapsed to the ground, with a grunt of pain, Paulina tumbling from his arms.

"Fuck!" I screamed, my voice breaking the stillness of the night. At that very moment I instinctively fired back at the hit man. With each burst of fire, the gun jerked in my hand. With the return of my fire, the hit man quickly retreated, closing the front door behind him, but not before I managed to get off a few more shots.

Everything seemed like it happened in slow motion after I watched the door close. I turned my attention back to Neil as he clutched his bleeding leg. "We've gotta pull back," I told him, referring to retreating back to the side of my house as a shield.

At that moment Neil crawled back toward the side of my house, and I grabbed Paulina under the arms and dragged her to where Neil had found some cover. We all huddled together, panting and trembling, as the reality of our situation sank into our minds.

I could tell that Paulina was in more pain than ever, and the fact that Neil had been shot and wouldn't be able to function at his full capacity made our circumstances look bleak. I stood there, trying to figure out what we should do next. "I'm sure they knew you were hit, so it's a matter of time before they'll be out here on our asses."

"Yeah, we can't be out here like sitting ducks." Neil gasped, his face pale from the pain.

I knelt beside Neil, checking his leg. The bullet had gone clean through, and he was losing a lot of blood. "We need to stop the bleeding," I said, tearing a strip of fabric from my shirt and tying it around his leg as a makeshift tourniquet.

Neil winced, but nodded.

After I stood back up, my mind started racing. I couldn't let Lacey's hit man come out and ambush us, especially while we were in this vulnerable position. I mean, Neil didn't have to come all the way out here to check on me, but he did, and now he's out of commission, so I've gotta do something. After mulling over the different scenarios of how Lacey's hit man could come out here and kill us, I quickly came up with a plan and sprang into action.

"Be right back," I said hastily, because I knew I had to confront Lacey and her hit man directly.

I heard Neil whisper behind me, "Where are you going?"

I couldn't answer him, because if I did, he'd try to stop me.

"Be careful," he murmured, his words barely above a whisper. Nevertheless, I heard them.

With that notion I jetted off to the back of my house. It was the only way to ensure their safety. I nodded unconsciously as I steered myself to the side door that led to my garage. Once I was standing directly in front of it, I took a deep breath, grabbed the spare key from underneath the pile of stones that were strategically placed there by me for an occasion such as this. I carefully pushed it into the lock of the doorknob, twisted as quietly as I could, and then I pushed the door open gradually, making sure I didn't make a sound.

Immediately after I assessed that no one was inside, I crept into the garage and closed the door behind me. Right after I closed the door, I firmly held Neil's gun steadily in my hand. I took a few steps farther into the garage, my senses on high alert as I listened for any movement that would come from inside the house.

As I moved toward the door that separated the garage from the kitchen, I placed my ear to it and held my breath to prevent being heard, and then I listened intently for any voices coming from inside the house. After standing there for a few seconds, I heard something. When I closed my eyes, I realized that it was voices.

"Did you get them?" I heard Lacey ask.

"Whoever that guy was carrying the housekeeper, I shot him and dropped him to the ground." The hit man's voice was low and terrifying.

"What about Ava? Did you get her?" Lacey wanted to know.

"I tried, but she took shelter behind that guy."

"Ugh! So she got away, yet again?" Lacey sounded frustrated.

"They can't be far. They've gotta be somewhere laying low around the house, because when I first started shooting at them, they were trying to get to that car down by the end of the driveway."

"I'll tell you what, if she manages to escape, you won't get the rest of your money," I heard Lacey say, her voice was sharp and angry.

"I'll find her, don't worry," the hit man replied.

"Then go! Because I need to get what I came here for. Don't come back until she's dead," Lacey instructed.

My heart pounded as I heard footsteps approaching. I stood still, hoping that Lacey's hit man wouldn't enter the garage to exit the house. But, sadly for me, that was not my reality. When Lacey's hit man grabbed the doorknob of the garage door and started twisting it gradually, I shot away from the door and hid behind the tail end of my car. My timing could not have been more perfect.

Unfortunately for Lacey's hit man, it was too dark in the garage for him to see me in the dark, but I could see him as he walked slowly between me and Paulina's car. He treaded cautiously, making sure that he didn't trip over anything. In my mind, though, he could've been making sure that no one else was inside the garage with him. Either way I remained quiet and still.

As he made his way toward the garage door that led to the outside, it dawned on me that I couldn't let him leave the house or he'd find Neil and Paulina. He'd kill them on the spot, so I jumped into action. I stood up on my feet very quietly, tiptoed behind him as he faced the side door, and then I took a deep breath, raised the gun, and aimed it at him. "Where do you think you're going?" I asked quietly.

Shocked by my presence, he tried to turn around, but I let off two shots before he had a chance to do anything.

POP! POP!

The bullets hit him square in the back, and he staggered forward, falling to the ground. The gun he had in his hand fell onto the garage floor and slid a few feet away from him. I approached his body cautiously; my gun still aimed at him. Before I grabbed his gun, I walked up to him while he was lying facedown and shot him in the head.

POP!

A few seconds later, blood pooled from his head and the chest area of his body.

I was sure that Neil and Paulina heard the gunshots and were probably worried that I was the person shot, but that was entirely the opposite of the truth. One part of me wanted to go outside and let them know that I was fine, but I had bigger fish to fry, and little time to do it, especially if my neighbors heard the gunshots, too, and decided that they wanted to call the cops. So I put Neil and Paulina on the back burner, grabbed the hit man's gun, stuck it in the waist of my pants, and then I headed toward the door that would let me back into my home.

After I entered my house, I moved quickly down the hallway, my footsteps silent on the hardwood floor. The closer I got to the staircase that led to the upstairs, I could hear that Lacey was rummaging through my things in my bedroom. This angered me. I mean, how dare this bitch come into my house, attempt to kill me, and then try to take what now belonged to me? Was she out of her damn mind? I wasn't going to let her leave this house with anything. And if she did, it would be over my dead body.

As I tiptoed upstairs, I kept Neil's gun raised and ready to let off another shot. It seemed like the closer I got to my bedroom, the more my adrenaline pumped through my veins. I finally made it to the top step and crept toward my bedroom. The door was slightly ajar. From my angle I wasn't able to see what she was doing, but I heard her movements loud and clear.

I carefully pushed the door open, because from what I was hearing, Lacey was now in my closet going through my things. After I opened my bedroom door wide enough for me to slip inside, I crept up to my closet door with the gun raised, stepping across all the things of mine that she tossed all over my room. As soon as I got to the doorway, I stood there and watched her go through all my handbags and then toss them onto the floor.

It was dark, but from the light of the outside street pole and the small flashlight she had gripped between the lips of her mouth, I could see that she had ransacked my entire closet. I noticed that she also didn't have a gun on hand, either. I knew then that I had the upper hand.

"You know I would make you clean up all this shit if we had time," I said, my voice cold and unwavering.

Lacey froze, then slowly turned around. Her eyes widened when she saw me standing there, gun pointed directly at her, and she chuckled. "I should've known that you weren't going to run and leave all of this money behind," she remarked.

"Why should I? It belongs to me now."

"No, it belongs to my brother and I'm taking it back," she said rather calmly. "Nasir, she's up here! Come and get her!" she yelled for her hit man.

I chuckled back at her. "Girl, he's not coming to save your ass! He's dead, and you're about to join him."

Lacey's eyes narrowed and her face twisted with rage. Without a moment's notice she tossed one of my handbags at me and then lunged. I stumbled backward, to keep her from attacking me, and then I let off two shots.

POP! POP!

The gunshots echoed throughout the house, the flashlight fell out of her mouth, and she tumbled forward.

BOOM!

And just like that, she hit the floor.

I snatched up the flashlight and searched high and low for Nick's laptop. I finally found it stashed in a tote bag that Lacey had placed on the floor near the entryway of my closet. I used that same tote bag and grabbed the money I had stashed in my safe, because I knew the cops would go through my things once they came here to remove the dead bodies. I couldn't leave any evidence behind of what I was involved in when the homicide detectives came in to start their investigation. I had too much to lose.

After I had Nick's laptop in hand, gathered everything from my safe, plus the gun I purchased from Neil the day before and the case that it came in, I headed back outside the house, where I left him and Paulina. From the looks of things, they were barely holding on, but were relieved to see me.

"Come on, let's get you guys to the hospital," I said after I approached them.

"Thank God you're okay! I thought you were dead!" Paulina said.

"I thought the worst, too," Neil admitted.

"Well, I'm not. So let's get out of here," I said as I helped Neil to his feet, supporting him as best as I could.

"Paulina, I'm gonna get him to the car first and then I'll come back for you, okay?"

"Sure," she replied.

Immediately after I escorted Neil to the car, I got in the driver's seat and drove it back up my driveway. After I managed to get Paulina in the backseat, I slid into the driver's seat, my hands shaking around the steering wheel.

Neil saw this and said, "It's okay. You got it."

I smiled at him and replied, "You're right"; then I put the car in reverse, floored the gas pedal, and backed out of the driveway in a flash of lightning. When I reached the street, I put the car in drive and pressed down on the gas pedal again, screeching the tires on Neil's car and sped away from my house.

As I drove away, I glanced back through the rearview mirror, the dark silhouette of my house reminding me of the dead bodies that were lying around ominously in the darkness. That alone gave me an eerie feeling inside, and the thought of me and the kids never living there again crossed my mind. There was no way I would be able to continue living there knowing that my husband died there, along with Nick's cohorts.

I was a spiritual person, and I know that bad spirits roam. I want to live in peace, and the chances of me doing that—with people I killed—wouldn't be possible. So, with that, I started thinking about other living arrangements. But for now, I had to get Neil and Paulina to the hospital before I lost them, too.

While heading out of my neighborhood, I saw two police cars rushing in my direction. My heart nearly jumped out of my chest, while sweat instantly poured from the pores of my hands.

Neil lifted his head up from the headrest. "Looks like one of your neighbors called the cops."

"Should we stop?" Paulina asked, her words barely audible.

"No, we gotta keep going," I told her. Because I wasn't about to stop this car, it would've been too risky. If they found all the money I stashed in Neil's backseat, it would've been hard to explain to them what it was doing there, and I wasn't about to chance that. Not only that, I wasn't ready to answer anyone's questions. I wanted to do things my way and that was to drop these two off at the hospital and then go and get my kids.

CHAPTER 31

Ava

THANKFULLY, IT ONLY TOOK ME ABOUT TEN MINUTES TO RUSH them both to the hospital. The moment we pulled up to the emergency entrance, I hopped out of the car, got the attention of two paramedics putting supplies in the back of the ambulance, and had them help take both Neil and Paulina inside. The part that annoyed me was when they started asking me questions. I yelled and told them that Paulina was my housekeeper, and she had been shot by a group of intruders who had entered my home. After I said that, I hopped back into Neil's car and raced over to the hotel my dead husband had the kids holed up at.

On my way to the hotel, I realized that I didn't get Kevin's hotel room key from his pants pockets. Since I couldn't turn back around and go home, I decided to go with plan B and that was to ask the hotel desk clerk to call his room and pray that one of the kids would answer the phone.

During the drive I also prayed that my babies were safe and sound. Knowing Lacey like I did, she could have had someone sitting with them while she manipulated Kevin into bringing her to my home to rob and kill me. I just hoped that wasn't my kids' reality.

Finally, after driving another fifteen minutes to Kevin's hotel, I pulled into the parking lot, and my heart instantly started pounding the moment I spotted three cop cars parked outside the entrance. The flashing lights reflected off the building, making the situation feel even more surreal.

"Please don't let this have something to do with my kids," I uttered quietly.

Immediately after I parked Neil's car, I climbed out of it and locked the doors so that no one could get inside; then I hurried inside the hotel lobby, anxiety tightening my chest. Immediately after I entered the lobby, my eyes landed on my children. Little Kevin and Kamryn were sitting on one of the lobby's sofas, talking to a white female cop, who knelt beside them, speaking softly. Next to them stood a short Black woman wearing a shoulder-length wig, dressed in plain clothes, her expression serious, but from where I was standing, I could tell that she was gentle. I raced over to where they were, and the moment the kids saw me, their faces lit up with relief.

"Mommy!" they both shouted as they jumped off the sofa and ran toward me. I dropped to my knees and held out my arms. When we connected, I wrapped them in a tight embrace.

"I'm here," I assured them, and for a brief moment the world outside of me ceased to exist. Unfortunately for me, the reprieve was short-lived.

The female cop walked over to where the kids and I were and gently placed a hand on my shoulder. "I take it, you're their mother?"

I looked up from my children and nodded.

"Well, ma'am, we need to speak with you," she said in a calm but firm tone of voice.

I released the kids from my embrace and stood up on my feet. "Give me a minute, you guys. And as soon as I'm done talking, we're gonna leave," I told them.

"Okay," they both said in unison.

As the female cop and I walked a few feet away from the kids, my mind started racing. "What's going on? Why are you here with my kids?"

"Well, first off, my name is Officer Coleman, and your son, Little Kevin, called us. He was worried because his father called the hotel room, around an hour ago or so, and told him he loved him and to never forget that, and then . . . nothing. Your son said he stayed on the phone waiting for his father to say something else, but he didn't. Then after waiting to hear something, he heard gunshots, got scared, and called 911, hoping that we could help his dad."

I looked over at Little Kevin, who was now back in the presence of what I presumed was the social worker, and my heart went out to him. There was no question in my mind that he heard the gunshots that were fired in my house. I wanted so badly to run over and hold him in my arms again.

"He also told us that his father went to your house, and with that information, we sent two patrol cars over there," she added, and I felt a large lump form in my throat.

"Yeah, I saw them," I mumbled unconsciously.

"What do you mean, you saw them?" she replied, her expression got more serious. "You were there?"

"Look, I'm tired right now and all I want to do is take my kids and leave, if you don't mind," I said nonchalantly.

"Well, I'm sorry, that's not gonna happen, especially with you showing up here with your clothes soaked in blood," Officer Coleman pointed out. "Is that their father's blood on your clothes?"

My patience was beginning to run thin, and frustrated, I said, "No, it's not. It's my housekeeper's blood."

"Where is your housekeeper now?" Officer Coleman wouldn't let up.

"I dropped her off at the hospital."

"What hospital?"

"I don't know," I said, trying to jog my memory. "I think it's the one about fifteen minutes from here."

"Are you talking about Houston Methodist?"

"Yeah, that's the one."

"What's your housekeeper's name?"

"Paulina Acosta."

"What happened to Paulina?" Officer Coleman's questions continued.

I let out a long sigh, dreading to answer this lady's question. "She was shot."

"Did you shoot her?"

"No, I didn't," I snapped. When I raised my voice, every officer, my children, the social worker, and the bystanders looked in my direction.

"Who shot her?"

"The people who came to my house to kill me."

"Who tried to kill you?"

"Listen, ma'am, my body is tired and aching. I can't think straight right now and all I want is my kids so that I can leave," I explained.

"I'm sorry, but I can't let you take your children and leave."

"So you're gonna stop me!" I roared. In my mind this lady was tripping out. She had no idea what I had just gone through back at my house. I hadn't done anything wrong. I hadn't killed anyone who didn't try to kill me first. Not to mention, all I wanted to do was get my kids and just be with them alone.

Officer Coleman immediately held up her right hand, blocking my path, and then she used her left hand to get the attention of other police officers to assist her. "Hey, Maverick and Sams, I need you," she called out, and I noticed two white cops coming at us.

"So, what are you about to do, arrest me now?" I asked her, frustration filled my face.

"No, we're just gonna take you downtown and ask you a few

more questions so that we can get a better understanding about what's going on," she explained.

"Look I told you everything," I assured her.

Officer Coleman's eyes zoomed back on my blood-soaked clothes. "Judging by your clothes, I'm sure there's more to the story."

"What about my kids? Are they coming with me?"

"No, I'm afraid not. Mrs. Sherman is one of our most respected social workers and she's going to take them into her custody until we can iron this situation out."

Before I could utter another word, the crackle of the police radio interrupted me. "This is unit 7, we found multiple deceased bodies at the home address you dispatched," a voice reported.

Hearing a male's voice report the bloodbath at my home made me feel warm all over; I felt the room spin as the weight of the words sank in.

Deceased bodies. My home.

I knew there was no way that I was going to be able to talk myself out of this one, so I just stood there in despair while Officer Coleman's expression hardened. She reached for her handcuffs.

"Ma'am, please turn around," she didn't hesitate to say.

"No, wait!" I still managed to protest, my voice shaking as I was forcibly turned and handcuffed behind my back. I couldn't do anything else but look over at my children, who were now watching the scene unfold with wide, terrified eyes. "Please let me just . . ." I tried to say, but Officer Coleman was already tightening the cuff around my wrists. Seconds later, she started reading me my rights, and Mrs. Sherman, the social worker, casually guided Little Kevin and Kamryn away.

"Mommy!" Kamryn cried out first, trying to break free, but the social worker held her firmly.

"Where are y'all taking my mom?" Little Kevin sprinted off in my direction, but before he could get within three feet of me, Officer Maverick grabbed him.

"Get off me! Get off me!" he snapped, trying to fight the cop off him.

"Little Kevin, it's okay, baby. I will be all right," I shouted loud enough for him to hear me, hoping at the same time that my words would console him.

Unfortunately, my words fell on deaf ears and Little Kevin kept resisting the cop. This broke my heart because I couldn't do anything about it. Once again my heart shattered, and I felt powerless as my children were taken away from me.

While I was led out of the hotel lobby, my kids' cries echoed from behind and it damn near killed me. What was I going to do now?

CHAPTER 32

Ty

On Monday morning the sound of my cell phone ringing woke me up out of my sleep. When I looked at the screen, I registered it was a little after six, and the number calling me was an unfamiliar one. I wondered who this could be, but then I realized that I wouldn't know unless I answered the call.

"Hello," I said, curiosity consuming me.

"Hello, ma'am, this is Detective Morales calling from Houston Homicide Division. May I speak with Ty Peeples," a deep, authoritative voice said.

"This is she," I replied, my heart picking up speed, thinking the worst after he mentioned that he was calling from Houston Homicide Division.

"Hi, ma'am, can you tell me what relation is Kevin Frost to you?"

"Well, I'm his fiancée, we live together, and we just had a baby. So, can you tell me what this call is about? Is he all right?"

"No, ma'am, I'm afraid he's not. We found his body last night at his current wife's house," the officer informed me.

At that moment I froze, and the world seemed to stop spinning after the detective told me that Kevin was dead. But I managed to hold my cell phone with a firm grip as my mind struggled to process the words.

"Wait . . . did you say that you found his body at his wife's house?" I whispered, barely holding it together.

"Yes, ma'am."

My mind raced, memories flooding back to the recent tension between Kevin and me, the secrets he had kept from me and the dangerous situation in which he might have gotten himself involved. Without warning, my scream tore through the phone, raw and filled with anguish.

"No! No, no, no!" I cried out, my body shaking as the reality of the situation hit me like a tidal wave. "I knew she was going to kill him, I knew it." I continued to scream through the phone.

"Who are you talking about, Ms. Peeples?" the detective asked me.

"I'm talking about his wife, Ava," I blurted out, because I knew that I needed the cop to know what I knew about the situation.

"How do you know that his wife killed him?" he probed, his voice measured, trying to remain calm against my grief.

"Because I made a call to her a couple of days ago and told her that I heard Kevin on the phone with someone talking about possibly killing her and her housekeeper!" I yelled through the phone. The pain of knowing that I could've possibly caused Kevin's death was tearing me apart. I had to let it out.

"Who are the other people, Ms. Peeples?"

"I don't know. But I know Kevin left Virginia for the purpose of seeing his children and meeting those people," I explained more in depth.

"Ms. Peeples, do you think you could fly to Texas and have a meeting with me and my partner?" the detective asked.

"Of course, I can. I'm a flight attendant. I can hop on a flight today," I told him.

"Okay, well, take down my number and address and call me as soon as your plane lands."

"Will I be able to see Kevin's body?"

"I'm sure that we can make that happen."

After the detective gave me the green light, I took down his phone number and the address to the police department and reassured him that I would call him upon my arrival.

Before we ended the call, I asked, "Where is his wife, Ava?"

"She's in custody."

"Good," I said, and then I hung up.

After the call had ended, I sat there on the bed, sobbing uncontrollably, staring at my cell phone in my hand. My mind was swirling with thoughts, memories, and regrets. The life I had with Kevin was gone in an instant, replaced by a nightmare I knew was going to be hard to wake up from. Now that I was in this space of sorrow, I also knew that I needed to snap out of this state of mind—at least for the moment so that I could prepare and get myself on the next flight to Houston. But more than that, I needed answers—answers I feared might reveal more than I was ready to face.

After crying my heart out for the next thirty minutes, I called my best friend to tell her the bad news and see if she could take care of my little one while I flew out to Texas.

Whitney picked up on the second ring. "Hello," she answered.

I tried to formulate my words, but the weight of Kevin's death was beginning to suffocate me. Seconds later, the walls of my bedroom felt like they were closing in on me and I broke down in tears and started sobbing.

"Oh, my God! Ty, why are you crying?" She seemed very concerned.

"Whit, Kevin is dead," I said with finality as my voice wavered a bit.

"Wait, no, that can't be," she protested.

"I just got off the phone with a detective from Houston. He said that Kevin was found murdered at Ava's house."

There was a pause at the other end of the line, the silence filled with shock and disbelief.

"Oh, my God, Ty. I'm so sorry. I don't even know what to say."

Tears continued to fall from my eyes as I replayed the entire conversation I had with Ava a couple nights prior. "Whitney, I think this is all my fault. I called Ava and told her I overheard Kevin talking to someone about possibly hurting her. So, what if she took that information I gave her and decided to kill him?"

Whitney quickly interjected, "What did the cop say?"

"He told me they were still investigating what all happened."

"All right, so wait and see what they find out, and until then, don't go around blaming yourself for what happened out there."

"I understand what you're saying, but if I hadn't made that call, maybe Kevin would still be alive," I said, my voice breaking.

"Ty, listen to me," Whitney said, her tone leaving no room for argument. "Like I said, before you do anything, let the detectives conduct their investigation. You don't know all the facts yet. Blaming yourself isn't going to bring Kevin back, and it's not fair to put this on your shoulders. They'll find out what really happened."

"You're right, Whit. But I just . . . I feel so guilty right now," I confessed, wiping the tears from my eyes.

"I know you do, but you need to stay strong," Whitney reassured me, and then she asked, "So, what are you going to do? Wait until they do their investigation and wait for them to call, or are you going to go out there?"

"I told the detective that I was going to take the next flight out today."

"What are you going to do with baby girl?" Whitney wanted to know.

"I was calling you to see if you'd watch her for me, but then again, I wanted to take her with me," I replied between sniffles.

"Tell you what, if you pay for my flight, I'll fly to Houston with you. That way, I could be there to support you and help with the baby. I mean, I would hate to see you go through this alone."

"Thank you, Whit. I don't know what I'd do without you," I said after feeling a small sense of relief.

"No need to thank me. We're going to get through this together."

"Okay, well, start packing, and when you're done, head over here."

"Will do," Whitney said. "Hang in there, okay?"

"Okay," I whispered, feeling a little more grounded with her support. "I'll see you soon."

After we hung up, I took a deep breath, trying to steady myself, but at the same time dreading the emotional storm that lay ahead of me.

Immediately after I got off the phone with Whitney, I dialed my coworker Angela's cell phone number. She worked at one of the ticket counters for our airlines. "Hey, girl, you at work right now?"

"Yeah, what's up?"

"Are you with a customer?"

"Not at the moment. What do you need?"

"I need two flights to Houston today. The earliest ones you can find."

"Is everything all right?" she questioned after hearing the urgency in my voice.

"I just got a call from a homicide detective in Houston telling me that my boyfriend, Kevin, was found murdered in his soon-to-be ex-wife's house, so I'm trying to get on the next flight out there so that I can speak with the cops and make arrangements to bring his body back to Virginia."

"Awww . . . Ty, I am so sorry to hear that. Let me hang up and call you back from the help desk phone and then I'll be able to find you a flight."

I thanked her and ended the call. A minute later, Angela called back, and while she had me on the phone, she was able to squeeze Whitney and me on a one-way flight to Houston, Texas, leaving Richmond at eleven-ten this morning and arriving in Houston at one twenty-eight in the afternoon, Central Time.

I was so grateful for her helping me with this last-minute arrangement. After I told Angela how much I appreciated her, she told me not to mention it.

"Call me if you need anything else," she offered.

"I will, and thanks again."

"No problem. And safe travels."

After the flights were booked, I called Whitney back.

"Hey, girl, I got the flights, and it departs Richmond International at eleven-ten this morning, so as soon as you pack, just head on over here. I wanna be at the airport at least by nine o'clock."

"I'm on it," she affirmed.

"Thanks, girl," I responded.

"You know I got ya back and we're gonna get through this together."

"That sounds easier said than done, but okay," I remarked before ending the call.

CHAPTER 33

Ava

I COULDN'T FREAKING BELIEVE THAT I WAS SITTING IN THIS COLD-ASS room, handcuffed to a table; there was a security camera mounted in the corner watching my every move. Of course, I was no stranger to being behind bars, but it had been years since my last stint. I had to admit that a lot of things had changed since then.

Now, being here wasn't the problem, because I could handle this environment. The part I couldn't handle was having my children in someone else's care while I was here. God knows what they're going through, or what was going on in their minds right now, and that alone was breaking my heart.

I couldn't tell what time it was, but I'd been in this shithole for at least twelve hours, answering tons of questions thrown at me by these homicide detectives. I was exhausted, to say the least. From the time I arrived, they stuck me in this room and started asking me all sorts of questions. I believe I told them every detail, from start to finish, of how Kevin just popped up at my home to get the kids, to taking them with him to the hotel for the weekend, and then showing back up with Lacey, Maceo, and their hit man a day later to kill me. I refused to tell them about the money and the laptop, though.

There was no way I was going to give away that information, jeopardizing my financial security. No way. So, when they asked me why would Kevin bring those people to my home to kill me? I told them he and I were going through a divorce, and he probably wanted to get rid of me so that he could get my life insurance policy and be awarded the home we now have on the market in Virginia. At the end of the interrogation, I told them my story could be corroborated by my housekeeper, Paulina, and a friend. After I gave them Neil's full name and told them that I had dropped him off at the hospital, along with my housekeeper, they told me that they'd get back to me and left me alone in this room. That was a few hours ago.

While all the movement was going on outside this room, I still found a way to think about how I was going to get out of this shit, if they decided to charge me with Lacey's and her hit man's murders. I was new in this town, so I had no idea who would be the best attorney for this type of problem I had. Maybe I'd get Neil to refer me to someone.

Not to mention, I was going to need a new place to stay, if and when they let me out of here. There was no way I was going to stay in that house with my kids after all the bloodshed that went on there. I couldn't have haunted spirits of Lacey, Maceo, and her hit man roaming around my house while I'm asleep at night. No, I can't have that happen.

As every possibility of how my life would be, from this day forward, crossed my mind, I heard keys jangling from outside the door and then I saw the door open. It was one of the detectives who had interrogated me. He walked over to where I was sitting and began unlocking the handcuffs from my wrists.

"Today is your lucky day," he said.

I sat up in the chair as hope filled my heart. "What do you mean?" I wanted clarity.

"My partner and I just left the hospital and spoke with your housekeeper and your friend Neil. They both corroborated your story."

"So you're letting me go?"

"Right now, we are, but we will continue on with our investigation. If we find out anything different, we will come back for you."

I didn't waste any time standing up on my feet. I was ready to get out of there before he changed his mind. So, as I made my way to exit the room, the detective walked ahead of me and instructed me to follow him, so I did. He led me down a long, narrow corridor, each step seeming to come faster than the last. I was so ready to get out of there.

After walking down another hallway, we finally made it to the main lobby of the precinct and I was shown the EXIT door.

"Because this is an ongoing investigation, you're not to leave town. Understood?"

"Yes, I understand, but can you tell me where my children are?" I replied.

"I'm not sure, but if you call Harris County Family Services, on Chimney Rock Road, and ask for Mrs. Sherman, she'll be able to help you," he stated.

"Will I be able to pick them up from their office?" I continued to question him.

"I can't answer that, but if you call their office, they will be able to give you that information," he said with little-to-no interest.

"Yeah, a'ight," I said with frustration, and then I left the building.

The bright daylight temporarily blinded me, so I squinted my eyes trying to adjust to the outside world. The fresh air made me feel a sense of freedom, and from this point on, nothing else was going to hold me back.

* * *

Under normal circumstances I would not have resorted to asking a total stranger for a ride, but I did today. While walking through the parking lot of the police station, I saw an older gentleman wearing a janitorial uniform getting into his car. I walked over to where his car was parked and asked if he could take me to the hotel I was picked up from the night before. This way I could get my car, and, to my surprise, he happily obliged.

He told me his name was Edward Johnson and that he had worked at the police station as a janitor for fifteen years. I lied and told him my name was Paulina and the cops brought me down here to the police station to question me about a robbery. I was shocked that he didn't pry into the details of this so-called robbery. He seemed to be more interested in where I was from, because it was obvious that I didn't speak like a Texas native.

"I'm from Virginia," I told him.

"How long you been living here in Houston?"

"About four months now."

"Like it here?"

"Yes, I do," I insisted, in spite of the fact that I had just endured a horrific night of killing and bloodshed. But he didn't need to know that, and I wasn't about to tell him.

We continued our small talk until we reached the hotel where I had left Neil's car parked the night before. Thankfully, it was still there and parked in the same place I left it. After I thanked the man for the ride, I got out and climbed into Neil's car. Immediately after I started up the ignition, I put the car in drive and headed straight to the Child Protective Services office on Chimney Rock Road.

When I arrived at the building, my heart started pounding uncontrollably, but I was able to remain cool as I approached the reception desk in the lobby. A young Black woman, who looked to be in her late twenties, with a friendly but professional demeanor, was seated behind it. I took a deep breath and walked up to her. "I'm here to see Mrs. Sherman." My voice was pleasant and calm.

"Your name?"

"Ava Frost."

"Is she expecting you? Because this is around the time she goes to lunch," the young woman told me.

"I don't have an appointment, if that's what you're asking. But she took my children from me last night and I'm here to pick them up."

The receptionist nodded and picked up the phone. "I'll let her know you're here. Please have a seat."

"Okay," I said, and then I turned around and walked over to a group of empty chairs a few feet away from the receptionist's desk. There was absolutely no one else in this lobby area waiting to be seen, so I chose a chair near the window, my mind racing the entire time.

Sitting there, I had time to think about all the mistakes I made that led to this horrific event. There was no way I should've walked into the lobby of the hotel with this bloody shirt on. If I hadn't, maybe the cops would not have questioned me the way they did, and I would've been able to walk out of there with my children last night.

I also couldn't help but think about how traumatic this whole experience has been for my children. First, the kidnapping, and now this, and both times it was all Kevin's fault. If he hadn't owed Nick all that money, Nick would not have had my children taken from me. And then this bullshit happened—with Kevin taking my children from the house and leaving them in a hotel so that he could bring Lacey and her goons to my home to rob and kill me. I mean, what's next?

As I sat there in deep thought, I realized I had been there for three and a half hours, and I wasn't liking it one bit. It didn't take this long for her to take my children away from me. Why was it taking her so long to see me? I stood up and walked back over to the receptionist's desk.

"Excuse me, but is she back from lunch yet? And if so, can you tell me how much longer I'm gonna have to wait? I mean, I've been here for three and a half hours now. It's three thirty-four."

"I'll check for you," the young woman volunteered, and picked up the phone once again. "Mrs. Sherman, Ava Frost wants to know how much longer you will be?" she spoke into the phone. "Okay, I will let her know," she added, and then she hung up the call. "She said she'll be with you in a few minutes."

"Thank you," I replied, and walked back over to where I was sitting.

After I took a seat, I waited about five minutes; then the door at the far end of the lobby opened and Mrs. Sherman stepped out, with sharp eyes and a composed expression.

"Mrs. Frost," she called my name, and gestured for me to come to her.

I stood up from the chair and walked over to where she was standing. When I got within arm's reach of her, she said, "Please follow me."

Without saying a word, I followed her down a long hallway, and I couldn't help but notice the sound of her footsteps echoing off the walls. Mrs. Sherman led me into a modest office, decorated with family photos, a few motivational framed quotes, and some framed Afrocentric art. She closed the door behind us and offered me a seat before settling into her own chair behind the desk.

After I sat down, I didn't waste any time. "Where are my children?" I demanded to know.

Mrs. Sherman met my gaze, her expression unreadable. "Your children have been placed with a very trusted foster care family until we can get some things resolved," she finally said.

My eyes widened in disbelief. "Come on, lady, please don't tell me that you put my children in foster care. Now I'm about to crash out in here," I commented, losing my patience.

Mrs. Sherman took a deep breath, her tone calm and measured. "Listen, Mrs. Frost, I know how difficult this is right now—" she started to say, but I cut her off.

"No, you listen, just tell me where my kids are so I can go and get them. I'm tired of talking about this," I snapped.

"Mrs. Frost, I'm afraid it's not gonna be that simple."

I shot up from the chair in a panic. "So you telling me that I *can't* get my kids back?" I raised my voice at her.

Mrs. Sherman stood up from the chair behind her desk, as if she was standing her ground, too, but remained calm. "I'm not saying that you can't get them back. All I'm saying is, there are serious concerns that need to be addressed first."

"What concerns? I spoke to the cops already and they let me go. So, what's the problem now?" I was still on high alert.

"Can you please have a seat?" she asked me politely.

"Look, I don't want to sit down, lady. I just want *my* kids!" I shouted.

Still handling the situation in a calm and gentle manner, Mrs. Sherman sat back down, hoping that I'd follow suit, but I didn't. I stood there, with my eyes blazing red, because she wasn't saying anything I wanted to hear.

"I spoke with Little Kevin at length after he expressed worry about you being arrested. He initially thought the police officers were taking you away because of a guy named Nick, who was killed. After further talking with him, he told me about the kidnapping he and his sister endured, which resulted in the murder that happened before you guys moved here to Houston. And the most damning part of his statement was that he was the one who actually shot and killed Nick with a gun that was on the floor of Nick's home," she recited to me.

Hearing her talk about Nick, the gun, and the murder instantly made my head spin. The blood drained from my face and I was at a loss for words. But I knew that I couldn't just sit there and not say anything, so I immediately went into damage control.

"I know that you didn't believe that, right? He's a kid, and Little Kevin has a tendency to make up stories from time to time. I've always had problems with him telling lies . . . and making up stories," I finally said.

"Well, I thought the same thing, but Little Kevin's admission raised some significant concerns, so I reached out to the authorities back in your hometown. I spoke to the FBI and to Detectives Kelly and Mann about the kidnapping. They both are actively investigating the murder case of Nick Ross. And because of that, I made the decision to place them in foster care."

My anger flared instantly after hearing this lady tell me that she called the cops back in Virginia. "Are you freaking kidding me now? You had no right! I'm their mother! You should've spoken to me first."

Mrs. Sherman remained composed. "I'm sorry, Mrs. Frost, I was just doing my job. My priority is the safety and well-being of your children."

"I need to see them. I need to know they're okay," I said, my emotions surged, a mix of fear and frustration for my children.

Mrs. Sherman softened slightly, her eyes reflecting a hint of sympathy. "Look, I'll do everything I can to facilitate a visit. But for now, we need to make sure that the proper steps are taken to protect everyone involved."

"And when will that be?"

"I can't say."

"What do you mean, you can't say?" I snapped once again. "You can do what you wanna do. So pick that phone up and call those folks who have my kids and tell them that I'm coming over there to see them," I instructed her. I wasn't backing down. I'd had enough of this back-and-forth with this lady.

Just as Mrs. Sherman was about to speak again, a sharp knock echoed through the door.

Mrs. Sherman glanced toward the entrance, her expression tightening. "Excuse me for a moment, Mrs. Frost," she said calmly before standing and walking to the door.

I watched as she opened the door, revealing two uniformed officers standing sternly in the doorway. The sight of them sent a chill up and down my spine, and my heart pounded in my chest as the reality of the situation began to sink in.

One of the officers, a tall man with a stern demeanor, stepped forward. "Ava Frost, please stand up and turn around," he commanded, his voice leaving no room for argument.

I immediately looked at Mrs. Sherman. "What's going on? You called them on me?" I asked, but she refused to answer my question.

Without any warning the taller officer approached me, producing a pair of handcuffs. My eyes darted back to Mrs. Sherman, searching for an explanation, but she remained quiet.

"So you're just gonna ignore me?" I shouted at her. Once again she refused to answer my question. It made my blood boil. "You coward-ass bitch! You think I'm stupid! You kept me out there in that waiting room all that time so you could call the cops on me. You're a sneaking-ass bitch! You have no idea what you did when you interfered in my business. I go hard for my children. *So know that this ain't over!*" I roared as the officer fastened the cuffs around my wrists.

Once they had me contained, they guided me out of the office and out of the Child Protective Services building, each step feeling heavier than the last. After they placed me in the patrol car, they sped out of there quickly. The drive back to the police station seemed quicker than the night before. Nevertheless, I had arrived there again.

As we entered the station, I was ushered down into the department where I was questioned by homicide detectives hours before, and immediately my eyes were drawn to a familiar figure standing next to the detective who had released me earlier that morning. It was Ty, Kevin's mistress.

I clearly remembered her face from the photo I questioned Kevin about months earlier. My question was, what was she doing here? Was she here to help with my situation? I swear, I couldn't read her face after our eyes connected across the bustling room full of people. But then as I got closer to her, her face twisted with a look of anger, hurt, and betrayal, and she opened her mouth.

"Ava, I tried to help you, and you kill Kevin?" she accused, her voice ringing out, drawing the attention of every police officer and bystander in the vicinity. I was stunned by her outburst, and it hung in the air, heavy and inflammatory, leaving me momentarily speechless.

The room seemed to close in around me as whispers and murmurs began to spread like wildfire. I felt eyes on me from every direction and the judgment was palpable. And right before I could respond, the officers led her away.

They escorted me through a maze of hallways until they reached another small, windowless interrogation room and handcuffed me to the table. The door clicked shut behind me, plunging me into seclusion. I couldn't do anything but sink onto the stiff chair, the metal surface cold against my skin. Time seemed to stretch interminably as I waited for someone to come through the door.

Minutes ticked away, each one feeling like an eternity. I tried to remain calm, but my mind wouldn't stop replaying the events from the night before to this morning, questioning every decision and every word spoken. Not to mention, the situation that popped back up about Nick's death. My nerves were frazzled about that. But I couldn't blame Little Kevin; he thought that by confessing to the crime, he was helping me.

After what felt like hours to me, the door opened once more, and the same detective from earlier stepped inside. His expression was grave, and I could see the weight of the situation etched into the lines of his face.

"Ava, we have a situation," he began, his tone serious. "Chesapeake, Virginia, detectives will be arriving sometime later today to extradite you and your son, Little Kevin, back to Virginia. They are charging you two with the murder of Nick Ross."

"What? Murder? I haven't killed no one!" I spat, my heart racing.

The detective sighed. "Well, when they get here, you can explain that to them," he said, then closed the door shut.

I was left alone with my thoughts once more. The reality of being taken away, and the uncertainty of what lay ahead, was overwhelming. I glanced around the interrogation room, the walls seeming to close in on me, and I sank deeper into my chair, the weight of my shattered world pressing down on me.

Two hours passed in a blur of anxiety and fear. I couldn't shake the feeling that everything I knew was falling apart. The realization of my past had come back to haunt me. My efforts to get my children back after the kidnapping, and escaping to another state to start a new life with all of Nick's money, seemed to have backfired. And now my son and I are facing some serious charges.

What will happen with my daughter? And what will happen with my money and Nick's laptop? My brain couldn't come up with the answers, so I just sat there in defeat. My world was over, and I couldn't do anything but face the uncertain path that lay ahead.

If only I had done things differently.

Finally, the wait is over! What die-hard fans of The Wifey Series have been waiting for! Here's a sneak preview of the prequel to this extremely popular series by Kiki Swinson, *Wifey in the Making*

Prologue

"WHAT THE HELL DO YOU THINK YOU'RE DOING?" QUE SHOUTED from the entryway of the closet door.

Startled, I turned around, my back now facing the safe that contained over two hundred thousand dollars in cash and a 9mm Glock and it all belonged to my man Que. Not sure what to say, I stood there and looked dumbfounded because it was evident what I was doing when he walked up on me by surprise.

"Answer my fucking question, bitch! Why were you trying to open my safe?" he roared as his face became menacing.

My heart started pounding rapidly and before I knew it, words started spilling out of my mouth. "I was getting the gun." I lied and he knew it.

"You're a motherfucking liar! You're trying to rob me for my fucking money!" he shouted as he charged toward me. As soon as he came within arm's reach of me, he grabbed my throat with his right hand, instantly applying pressure against my windpipe, cutting off my airflow. I frantically tried to pry his hand away from my neck, but his strength was too much for me. Tears formed in my eyes and started falling down my face one after the other. The only thing left for me to do was fight for my life, so I mustered up what energy I had inside of me and began to punch and scratched up his face.

It seemed like the more I tried to fight him off, the more pressure he applied to my neck and before I knew it, everything around me was going dark and I started losing consciousness. Then suddenly, Que loosened his grip on my neck and a sharp flow of oxygen seeped through my windpipe as he slung me down to the floor. *Boom!* I hit the floor hard and got tangled up in the clothes hanging up inside the closet. I was disoriented and confused about what to do next, so I laid there, massaging my neck and hoped that he'd walk away. Unfortunately for me, that didn't happen, because as soon as I took another breath, he reached down, grabbed the collar of my jean jacket with both hands, snatched me up on my feet and pulled me close to his face. I stood there helpless as this six feet, four inch, 220 pound man held me up in the air a few inches off the floor. "You know I kill people who try to steal from me, right?" he said, his words cut through me like a knife.

"I swear, I wasn't trying to steal from you." I lied once more, hoping he'd somehow believe me.

"So, why were you trying to open my safe?" His questions continued as he gnashed his teeth.

"I told you I was trying to get the gun."

"Stop lying to me, Kira! You know I hate being lied to." His voice boomed as he pressed his nose against mine. That was just how close he was in my face.

"I'm not. I swear!" I pleaded with him.

"Tell me what you needed my gun for," he demanded to know.

"I was going up to the club with my homegirls and I wanted to be strapped just in case one of those chicks from Norfolk tried to start some shit with us," I replied, hoping he would buy into my lie.

"Yo', Que!" I heard a voice shout from a few feet away and immediately knew that voice belonged to Que's homeboy, Ricky. Que looked over his shoulder while he still held me up in the air, feet dangling off the floor. "What's up?" he said.

"Nigga, I can hear you from outside in the car," he told him.

"You think I care. This bitch is in here trying to steal my money," Que accused me.

"I swear I wasn't. I was trying to get the gun," I said, holding dearly to the lie. There was no way I was going to admit to trying to steal any of Que's money. He'd kill me if I did.

"Que, put her down, man," Ricky asked him politely. But Que wasn't trying to hear anything Ricky was saying and started laughing like Ricky had just said something hilarious.

"So, whatcha' taking up for this bitch now?" Que asked him. His facial expression changed to disdain.

"No, I'm not taking up for her," Ricky answered him.

"Then what is it?" Que's questions continued.

Ricky took a few steps closer to Que and said, "Just let her go."

While I was massaging the back of my head to ease the pain, Que started walking toward Ricky. It only took about five or six steps for them to come face-to-face with each other. I sat there and watched intently as Que started off by saying, "Yo nigga, tell me the truth, you like my bitch or something?"

Instead of answering Que's question, Ricky looked past him and said, "Kira, let's go."

Shocked by his direct response toward me and ignoring Que altogether, my heart started racing uncontrollably because Que had accused me of looking at Ricky on several occasions when he came around. He had also mentioned that he caught Ricky looking at me too in different settings, but I always shot the claims down. Fast-forward to now, the cat was about to be let out of the bag.

Taken aback by Ricky's response, Que snapped and said, "Nigga, why the fuck you think you can tell my girl to get up and go with you?"

"Shit nigga, you don't know what to do with her so I'm taking her from you," he replied and then he moved by Que and started walking toward the closet.

In a flash, Que lunged at Ricky while his back was turned and shouted, "Nigga, you think you're gonna disrespect me in my house!"

"Watch out!" I warned Ricky.

Ricky jumped back in the nick of time and dodged a punch from Que. Before Que had a chance to regroup and throw another punch, Ricky pulled a gun from the waist of his pants, pulled back on the chamber and aimed it directly at Que's face. "Get the fuck back or I'm gonna splatter your brains all over these motherfucking walls," Ricky threatened.

Feeling a massive amount of betrayal, Que stood there and stared at Ricky in a very alarming way. I knew this face and I figured that at any minute he was going to leap toward Ricky and try to take the gun from him. That was just how daring Que was. "So, whatcha' gonna shoot me now?" he asked Ricky.

"Just let me and Kira leave and shit ain't gotta get ugly," Ricky told him. Then he looked over at me and said, "Kira, get up and come with me."

I immediately stood up on my feet, reached down and grabbed my purse and then I eased my way out of the closet very carefully and stood behind Ricky. Que's eyes beamed down on me and if looks could kill, I would be a dead chick right now. "So, that's what we're doing, Kira? You're leaving with this nigga?" Que questioned me.

"Don't talk to him. Just back up out of the room," Ricky instructed me as he kept his gun aimed at Que. I started backing up out of the bedroom and this hit a nerve with Que.

"Nigga, you can't stop her from talking to me!" Que snapped

and then he leapt toward Ricky. As Que was coming at Ricky, I heard Ricky's gun erupt. *POP! POP!* I screamed and scrambled out of the bedroom. As soon as I arrived in the hallway, I heard a loud thud. At that very moment, I knew that Que had to be dead, and the thought of it freaked me out, so I ran down the staircase and out the front door because I refused to be a witness to a murder. Shit, I was only twenty-one years old, so this was too much to take on and I kept running.

CHAPTER 1

The Beginning

Before I was the wife of Ricky, the wealthy, Jamaican drug dealer and the owner of a hair salon, I was an only child who'd grown up in a single-family household in the projects. My mother struggled to keep a roof over my head, food in my mouth, and clothes on my back. But there was never a shortage of men running in and out of our small apartment in the projects. I learned early on that my mother suffered from low self-esteem. She tolerated mistreatment from men, and she normalized it on so many levels. You would think that if a woman was entertaining different men, that she wouldn't want for anything, but that wasn't the case with my mother. She allowed the men to sell her dreams, and she was always left with nothing after they had their way with her.

Seeing this growing up, made me see men in a different light. I developed a no-nonsense attitude early and vowed that I wouldn't ever allow a man to play me like the men my mother had relationships with. I remembered having my first boyfriend at seventeen. His name was Justin, and he was a twenty-year-old drug dealer from New York. He came out the gate buying me gifts, taking me shopping and getting my hair and nails done.

He set the stage for me and gave me the attitude that if a man rocked with you, he was going to make sure that you were good. But what I didn't realize in the beginning was that, if you accepted money and pricey gifts from a man, you'd eventually have to return the gestures on the backend.

After dealing with him for about a couple of months, he came to my mother's apartment and asked me to hold some drugs for him. So, I did. He gave me a small paper bag that had a sandwich bag inside of it filled with over a thousand heroin-filled capsules. I didn't know the value of it then, but I later found out that I had over fifteen thousand dollars' worth of drugs in my possession. Now if someone had ratted me out, the cops would've stormed our apartment, locked me and my mother up and gave us at least twenty years. The Commonwealth of Virginia didn't play about giving people stiff sentences for heroin. And I did this for him at least three to four times a week.

From there I started making drug runs for him. I remember the day he came to me and said, "Hey love, wanna make some real money?" I smiled and said, "What do I have to do? And how much am I making?"

"There was this chick that used to bring our stuff here from New York, but she doesn't want to do it anymore, so we're looking for someone new to do it," he explained.

"How much was she getting?" I asked.

"We paid her two grand per trip," he replied.

Hearing him tell me that I was going to make two thousand dollars just to carry drugs from one state to the next seemed easy for that type of money, so I said, "Okay, let's do it."

The next day, I hopped in the car with my boyfriend and his two boys, and we headed up to New York. We picked up the drugs, stashed them in my overnight duffle bag and then they dropped me off at Port Authority bus station. I hopped on the bus, and I arrived back in Norfolk, Virginia, less than twelve hours later. And just like that, I caught a taxi to my mom's apartment, and they met me there. After they made sure all the drugs were there, I got paid the two thousand I was promised, and I was happy. I did over one hundred more drug runs for them until it all stopped abruptly.

Fast-forward eight months later, narcotics detectives ran up on Justin and his crew while they were on the block and busted them with about two thousand dollars' worth of drugs and they all went to jail. My drug running money dried up and I was right back at square one, so guess what I did. I started doing hair on the side and became a shampoo girl at the hair salon where I got my hair done at.

One day I was working in the salon with the woman who owned it, Debra Morgan. Debra was my hair stylist, and she was the best in the Tidewater area. She was a light-skinned, pretty woman with a curvy figure. She was known for having men with money to take care of her. Every drug dealer from around the way used to stop in and say hello.

One day while I was shampooing one of Debra's clients, two guys walked into the shop.

One of guys I knew instantly, and his name was Bishop. He was a very attractive cat from New York, and he was messing around with Debra. He resembled the actor Micheal Ealy, with pretty colored eyes and caramel skin. All the chicks from the city wanted him, but he only had eyes for Debra. From what I heard around town and from Debra's mouth, he had a lot of money. As a matter of fact, word on the streets was that he supplied the entire city of Portsmouth. All the local guys either worked for him or they copped their drugs from him.

The other guy who accompanied him wasn't that cute. In fact, he was a medium and the average height of a guy, but his attire was on point. He was dressed in a Gucci sweatsuit and a pair of Gucci sneakers to match. I couldn't see his hair because of the fitted New York Yankee ball cap he wore. He and Bishop greeted everyone in the salon after they walked in. Bishop walked over to Debra's workstation while the other guy found a seat near the door. I continued to wash the client's hair and when I was done, I escorted her over to Debra's station, told her to have a seat and then I headed back over to the wash bowl so I could clean up a bit. On my way back to the wash bowl the guy said, "Think you could wash my hair next?"

I stopped and looked over my shoulder and said, "Do you have any hair?"

He pulled off his ball cap and showed me a completely bald head. I chuckled. "You have no hair to wash," I stated.

"Tell you what? How much would you charge me for a head massage?"

"Fifty dollars," I replied jokingly, knowing he would give me a side look.

"A'ight, let's do it," he answered cheerfully and hopped up from his chair.

Stunned by his answer, I said, "You serious?"

"Yes, I would pay you fifty dollars for your phone number," he continued as he walked towards me.

I swear, I didn't know what to say. This guy was pouring it on thick and it was obvious that he wanted my company badly. I smiled at him and told him to follow me.

"What's your name?" I asked him.

"Que. And what's yours?"

"Kira."

"Pretty name."

"Thank you. Now, have a seat right here," I instructed him after we arrived back at the wash bowl.

After he took a seat, I placed a towel around his neck and right when I was about to lean him back, the door to the salon opened and four narcotics cops dressed in plain clothes and police vests walked inside. Everyone in the shop turned around and looked at them. There were three White guys and a Black one, and they all looked like they were former Navy seals. "I'm glad that we have your attention. Where is Debra Morgan?" one guy stepped up and asked.

"I'm Debra." Debra announced herself as she stood at her station as she slightly held up her hand.

"Well Debra, I have a warrant signed by the judge to search your business for illegal drugs and firearms," he stated.

Debra walked toward the cop and demanded to see the warrant. He unfolded a white piece of paper, held it up in front of her face for a few seconds and then he handed it to her. After Debra took the warrant, she stood there and read it. Meanwhile the lead cop stood next to her and said, "I want everyone in here to stay where you are. Do not move until you are told to do so." And then he assigned the other three officers to search Debra's back office, the bathroom and the product and utility closet. I sat there in shock and wondered how in the hell they got a warrant to come and search a place of business for drugs.